THE
MOONLIGHT
MAN

THE

MOO

NLIGHT MAN

AN
APPLE
PAPERBACK

BETTY REN WRIGHT

SCHOLASTIC INC.

New York Toronto London Auckland Sydney

Mexico City New Delhi Hong Kong

No part of this publication may be reproduced in whole or in part, or stored in a retrieval system, or transmitted in any form, or by any means, electronic, mechanical, photocopying, recording, or otherwise, without written permission of the publisher. For information regarding permission, write to Scholastic Inc., Attention: Permissions Department, 555 Broadway, New York, NY 10012.

ISBN 0-590-25238-0

12 11 10 9 8 7 6 5 4 3 2 1   0 1 2 3 4 5/0

Printed in the U.S.A.   40

First Scholastic paperback printing, September 2000
The text type was set in 12/18 pt. Janson Text.
Book design by Dave Caplan.

For Lucille and Ruth and Dorothy,
who were there when the
fireworks started.

THE
MOONLIGHT
MAN

ONE

I tried keeping a journal once before, when I was twelve — writing is my very favorite thing — but it didn't work. I guess I didn't have much to tell. But now I'm fifteen, going on sixteen and, believe me, this time is different. I'll pretend I can see you — whoever you are, reading this — and tell myself you're really listening, not just waiting for me, Jenny Joslin, to stop talking so you can start. The thing is, I *need* you! I'm scared. Somebody has to listen.

It won't be my dad, that's for sure. I don't mean he walks away when I say something — he's not like that.

It's just that most of the time he and I have different ideas about what's important.

For instance, when our U-Haul turned into Crescent Lane this morning, I was really excited. One minute we'd been rumbling along the highway, and the next we turned onto this narrow road winding up-hill through thick woods.

"Hey, this is beautiful!" I said. "I didn't know we were going to live in the woods. Lucky us!"

Dad laughed. "The real-estate agent says the town is growing in the other direction. He's been trying to sell this hillside for years, but no one wants it." He shook his head as if the trees — all shimmery, delicate green in the June sunlight — were one more example of what was wrong with the world.

"Are there bears in these woods?" Allie wanted to know. She's my sister, age six. She scrunched down between us when she asked.

"No bears," I told her, fast. My dad said, "Bears or not, you keep out of there, Allison. I don't want you getting lost."

Allie sighed and leaned against me. Great! I thought. It was the kind of remark that could give her nightmares for a week.

We rounded one curve after another. When the road ended we were facing a green semicircle with five small houses arranged around it. A crescent, I thought, and I had this very strange feeling that I'd been there before. In a happy dream, maybe. The houses were nothing special, practically alike and a little shabby, but I *loved* them from that very first look. I felt as if they'd been expecting us! (That's exactly the kind of thing I can write in my journal but could *never* say to my dad.)

"Which one's ours?" I asked.

He pointed to the second house from the left. "No prize," he said, "but the best I could get for the money. Kromner was glad to rent it — three of the five were empty. Most people go for townhouses or apartments these days, if they are going to rent. But beggars can't be choosers."

"Dad, it's going to be really great here," I told him. "Who wants to live in another stuffy old apartment?"

"They aren't all stuffy or old," he said. "Just the ones we can afford."

We climbed out of the truck and looked around, the way we had on all the other first days in all the other places we had moved to since my mother died. In five and a half years we've moved seven times. After a month or two my dad always finds something wrong with where we are. I could tell him what's wrong — Mom isn't there — but he doesn't like me to talk about her. We're supposed to get on with our lives and put the past behind us, he says.

Uncle Ted — he's a friend who works with Dad at the hardware store — and a man named Terry came over to help unload the truck. They carried stuff in, and Allie and I opened the boxes and stacked dishes in the cupboards and hung clothes in the dinky closets. At least, that's what I did. Allie wandered around looking lost, clutching the brown teddy bear she's had since she was a baby. She thinks she remembers our mother giving her that bear, but that's impossible since Mom died a few months after Allie was born. She never lets me pack Sammy when we move; he has to ride to our new place on her lap.

"I can see a squirrel's nest from my bedroom window," she announced. "And there's a tire hanging from a tree. Isn't that silly?"

"That's a tire-swing," I told her. "The last people who lived here must have had kids."

She looked pleased. "But I don't want that picture in my room," she went on. "I don't know those boys."

I shook out a couple of pairs of pants and hung them in my closet. "What picture, goofy?" I said. "There aren't any pictures."

An hour ago we'd checked out the house

together — the living room that stretched across the front, the small dining room and slightly bigger kitchen, the extra-narrow staircase that led to three little bedrooms, and a really old-fashioned bathroom. It's such an ordinary, old-shoe kind of house; maybe that's why I love it. It's been waiting for people to appreciate it, and we're the ones who will. Giggling, we'd decided who would have which bedroom. All the walls had been as bare as a bone.

Allie didn't argue. She hardly ever does. She just curled up at the foot of my unmade bed and twisted a lock of her thin brown hair until I gave up.

"Okay," I said. "Show me." She stood and led the way down the hall to the back room she'd chosen. There was no picture.

"It *was* right there," she said stubbornly. She pointed to a place near the back window, and I saw a darker rectangle in the faded blue wallpaper.

Something had hung there once.

"What was the picture like?" I asked, trying to sound as if it was no big deal. Maybe if she had to describe it, she'd admit she hadn't seen it after all.

I should have known better. "Three boys in an old car," she said promptly. "A car with no top."

"A convertible?"

"I guess. The boys were smiling at the person taking the picture. One of them was waving." She frowned at the wall. "I'll put my Peter Pan poster there, okay?"

"Okay," I said. "When we figure out which box the posters are packed in."

The business about the picture made me kind of uneasy for a moment. But then Dad yelled from downstairs that the truck was empty and we were all going to McDonald's out on the highway, and everything was great again. The Joslins were making a fresh start.

Supper was fun. Uncle Ted told jokes and Dad was upbeat, the way he sometimes is for a little while after we move. On the way back, the twilight made Crescent Lane mysterious, like a forest trail in a story. When we reached its end, the lights in the houses had a warm, yellow glow. Actually, only two houses were lit — the ones at either end of the crescent were empty, and ours was dark. Still, it was the best feeling I'd had in a long time — coming home at last.

We'd all had enough unpacking for one day. Dad plugged in the television set and settled in his recliner to watch a Brewers game. I decided to go for a walk, and Allie said she'd come, too. I don't know if she was still thinking about the picture in her bedroom, but she clutched my hand pretty tightly when we went outside.

"Who lives there?" she asked and pointed to the house on our right. It was exactly like all the others — two stories high, a narrow front porch, a little gable above the porch. A one-car garage in the back. The windows were dark and bare.

"Nobody, now," I told her.

"It looks lonesome," she said. "I hope someone moves in soon."

We turned left and walked toward the three other houses. The one next to ours had a small lamp in a living room window, and we could see figures moving on a television screen. The house beyond that was full of light. Country-western music drifted through open windows.

"Somebody's painting," Allie said. We watched a youngish-looking man balancing on a ladder in the living room, with a paintbrush in one hand and a soda can in the other. Soon a really pretty girl came in and stood looking up at the wall with her hands on her hips.

"It's orange," Allie commented, and it certainly was. That wall was the brightest, orangest orange I'd ever seen. It made me blink, just looking at it. The girl said something, and she and the painter laughed. You could tell by looking at them that they laughed a lot.

"Come on," I said finally. "We shouldn't spy on people. Besides, I want to walk around our own backyard before it gets too dark. You can try the swing if you want to."

"Maybe tomorrow," Allie said nervously. I told her she could go inside if she'd rather, but she clung to my hand tighter than ever.

There was no sidewalk around our house, just the narrow gravel driveway that led to the garage. When we reached the backyard, the moonlight showed the way to the swing. Even in the dark you could tell that the lawn was scraggly, with lots of dug-up spots where squirrels had been busy.

"This is going to be like living in a park," I said. There were no fences on the crescent, just a wide curving stretch of lawn enclosed by woods.

I tugged on the chain that held the tire-swing and sat in it myself before I let Allie try it. Then I pushed her very gently, because I knew Dad would want to check the chain in the daylight. As I pushed, I looked over at the yard next door and wondered if someone would move in there soon. Someone neat. I hoped so.

Allie began to hum, which is what she does when she's contented. It was the only sound, except for the insects chirping, the squeak of the chain, and very faintly, the painting people's radio. I looked at the open windows above our kitchen sink and wondered if we'd have time to buy curtains and put them up before Dad decided to move again. Then I glanced at our little back porch. It looked as if someone was sitting on the top step. Allie saw him at the same time and stopped humming.

It seemed to me the person was a man, or maybe a tall, skinny boy. He was leaning forward, his elbows on his knees and his chin resting on his fists. A small shape crouched beside him.

I grabbed the swing and held it still.

"Who's there?" I said. At least, that was what I meant to say. What came out was a froggy croak.

The man — if there really was a man — stood up and sort of drifted across the yard and around the side of the house. A dog — if there really was a dog — followed him. They were both just shadows, hardly darker than the other shadows around them.

Allie slid off the swing and leaned against me. "Did you see someone on the porch?" she whispered.

"I don't know," I told her honestly. "I think I did,

9

but now I'm not sure." I tried to keep the shakiness out of my voice. "It could have been a trick of the moonlight, I guess."

Allie took a deep breath. "Yup," she said. "That's what it was — a moonlight man and a moonlight dog." She started pulling me toward the house. "Jenny, can I sleep with you tonight?"

"If you promise not to kick."

So that's how it is. Allie's asleep, crosswise on my bed, while I write this. I hope you're listening. If you are, maybe you can tell me how a person can be happy to be in a place and be scared silly at the same time.

TWO

Here are some facts I've learned in just one week:
Number One: Our closest neighbors, the
Carpeks, are old and crabby. Mr. Carpek mutters
under his breath when he walks, and Mrs. Carpek always looks as if she smells something nasty. Both of
them are good at pretending they don't know anyone
new has moved into the crescent. Yesterday Allison
asked Mr. Carpek if he had grandchildren who might
come to visit, and he said, "No and glad of it."

Number Two: The painter with the orange walls is
Mike Burton, and his wife is Kathy. Actually, there's
only one orange wall; the rest of their living room is

creamy white. They have blue-and-green deck chairs and a striped futon instead of normal furniture. Their coffee table is a battered old trunk that belonged to Kathy's ancestors. It's a really beautiful room.

When we visit the Burtons — three times so far — I come home knowing what I want my life to be like. I want to look like Kathy, even though my hair is sort of streaky brown, not black. I want a husband as handsome and funny as Mike, and I'm going to make our coffee mugs in a pottery class. Dad says we're being pests, but when we leave, Kathy always says, "Come back soon, you two." I love the way she says it.

Number Three: Someone else is in our house, besides my dad and Allie and me.

Sounds crazy, I know, and that's why I made it Number Three. If I'd made it Number One you'd think you're reading the journal of a hysterical child, which I'm not. I may be fifteen, but I'm quite mature for my age. What I'm telling you here are facts.

Last Tuesday, Allie and I ate lunch in the backyard, and afterward, when I went inside for more cookies, I heard whistling. I wasn't scared at first — the sound was soft and sweet, like a flute. It took me a while to realize it was right there in our house. I stood in the back hall for a few seconds, and then I stepped into the kitchen — just one step, ready to run. The whistling came from upstairs. I said, "Who's there?" and the whistling stopped.

Just as I started to breathe again, I heard footsteps overhead. They were fast, heavy steps, like someone pacing. And there was another sound, too — sharp little clicks — the noise of a dog's toenails on bare wood.

I had put out a hand to pick up the phone, but when I heard the dog I decided calling 9-1-1 would be a waste of time. A burglar doesn't bring along his dog, right? I don't think he'd whistle while he worked, either. I grabbed a handful of cookies and went back outside.

Starbuck School, where Allie will go this fall, is only a few hundred feet away from our house. The main approach is a road leading up from the other side of the hill; from our side you can follow a path through the woods to the playground. This was a good time to check it out. I took Allie's hand and practically ran the length of the yard.

The path was short and easy to follow. In a minute we were out in the sunshine again, facing a wide playground, a baseball diamond, swings, and lots of neat stuff to climb on. Beyond them was the school, a two-story red brick building with paper cutouts taped on the windows.

Allie dropped my hand and headed across the diamond. A couple of kids were already on the swings, kicking up dust with their toes. They hardly glanced at her when she joined them, but I knew she would be all right. She may be shy, but she always manages to make friends. She's had lots of experience.

I dropped to the grass, cross-legged, and waited for my knees to stop shaking. Dad always says, "Take deep breaths when you want to calm down," so I tried that. Then I counted to thirty-eight by halves — one, one and a half, two — which is how old my mother was when she died. Her life seems longer when I count that way. I reminded myself that she must have had all kinds of things happen to her in thirty-eight years — wonderful things, sad things, really weird things. Probably much more weird than moving into a haunted house. It's nothing, she'd say, if I could talk to her. It's *your* house now.

After a while, the quivery feeling in my stomach went away. The sun felt like an arm across my shoulders and my eyes began to close, till the schoolyard was just a strip of golden light. Very far away, Allie giggled. She has a great giggle.

The next thing I knew, she was kneeling in front of me, patting my hand. "You were asleep," she said, giggling some more.

"No, I wasn't," I told her, but when I looked around I saw long shadows across the grass. The playground was empty.

"You looked so funny, sleeping sitting up," Allie said. "Like that kind of doll that bounces back up when you knock it over."

"I don't think I'd bounce," I said, getting to my feet. But I would. If I were a doll, that's the kind I'd want to be.

I began to feel sort of quivery again as we headed back through the woods, but the moment we stepped into our yard I felt better. The house looked as if it were waiting for us, just as it had the day we moved in.

"You left the door open, Jenny," Allie scolded. "Maybe a burglar got in!" But she didn't believe it, and neither did I.

The moonlight man doesn't have a chance, I told myself. It's our house now.

THREE

Our house.

I read once that there are holy men in India who *never* stop praying. They work and eat and go to the bathroom, and always, inside their heads, they are repeating the same special prayer-words over and over. I didn't think that was possible, but it is.

Our house — those are *my* special words. I wake up hearing them, at the same time some faint movement in the air makes me think an intruder may have just slipped out of sight. I say them out loud in the middle of the afternoon, when the footsteps begin upstairs and my heart thuds so hard I can barely breathe. I think them in the evening, when Allie and I are doing dishes and from the windows above the sink I see a tall man-shadow and its small follower drift across the far end of the yard. No matter what, this is our house!

Today I was planting flowers in the backyard, when Allie came tearing around the corner. She was clutching Sammy, and her face was shiny with excitement.

"They're here!" she yelled. "The new people!" She said it as if we'd been expecting them, and maybe we had. Our house needed neighbors.

I let her drag me along the driveway, and sure enough, a moving van stood in front of the house next door. A ramp was already in place, and while we watched, the movers began carrying furniture from the truck. A stocky, red-faced man in a business suit bustled back and forth giving orders that no one seemed to be listening to, and from inside the house a woman's high voice repeated, "Be careful! Watch out! Don't drop it!"

Most of the furniture they carried in was wrapped in layers of padding, but here and there you could see a part of a table leg or the arm of a chair. Every piece had a sunny, expensive glow. Antiques, I thought. No wonder the owners were worried about it.

"There's a girl, too," Allie said proudly, as if she'd arranged this whole scene. "She's still in the car."

We went up on our porch where we could see a gray sedan across the street, partly hidden by the van. No one seemed to mind our nosiness or even notice us sitting on the steps. After a while the movers went deep into the truck and stayed for a few minutes, talking in low voices. When they appeared again they were guiding an upright piano between them. It was all padded and strapped and looked as if it weighed a ton.

"Now you be careful with *that!*" the man in the business suit exclaimed. He stepped back, as if he didn't want to be near the ramp when the piano came down.

The car door opened and the girl stepped out. She wore my kind of clothes — shorts and a baggy T-shirt — but they looked better on her because she wasn't flat-chested and she stood so straight. Like a model, I thought, watching her watch the movers. Her face was very still, as if she were listening to something we couldn't hear, and she had a thick black braid that hung almost to her waist. As the movers lowered the piano down the ramp, she crossed the street toward them. I thought, I wouldn't want to be the one who lets that piano slip.

"It's valuable," she said, in a cool, clear voice. The men looked at her and nodded. Slowly, steadily, they edged the piano to the ground and carried it into the house. The girl and her father went in after them.

"She didn't say hello." Allie sounded disappointed.

"That's because she was worried," I told her. "The piano's important to her, the way Sammy's important to you. She'd have carried it on her lap if she could."

We watched for a while longer, until the movers folded up the padding that had protected the furniture and swung the ramp into the bed of the truck. Finally, just as they drove away, the girl came out of her house again.

"Hi," I called. "Welcome to the crescent." Maybe she'd noticed us before and maybe she hadn't, but I couldn't wait any longer.

"Hi," she said. Her voice was cool and sort of still, like the rest of her. "What's the crescent?"

I gestured at our semicircle of houses. "That's what I call it," I said. "Because it's at the end of Crescent Lane and all."

She nodded, sort of puzzled, and then we introduced ourselves. Her name is April Danner.

"We were hoping someone would move in pretty soon," I told her. "It's been kind of lonesome." She nodded again, and the puzzled look was still there. I wondered if she was going to ask, "What's *lonesome?*"

"We just moved here from the other side of town,"

I went on quickly. "We had lots of friends at our last place but —"

"Do you play?" she asked suddenly.

While I was trying to understand the question, Allie answered it. "Old Maid. Chutes and Ladders. Monopoly."

April laughed. "I meant —"

"She meant music," I said, giving Allie a squeeze. "Remember the piano? We don't play anything — sorry." Why was I apologizing?

"Well, I don't really play the piano much, either," April said. "It's not my true love." She stood up. "Stay here. I'll show you." She crossed the street again to the car.

"Do you like her?" Allie whispered. She rested her chin on Sammy's head.

"What's not to like?" I said. "Of course I like her."

April reached into the car, and when she turned around she was holding a violin case. She cradled it in both arms for a moment, as if it were a baby, and then she came back and opened it on a step below us. The violin gleamed like silk in the sunlight.

"It belonged to my great-uncle Frederick," she said softly. "He played with the Chicago Symphony. First chair. On his deathbed he told my mother he could die peacefully knowing I would love it as much as he did."

I didn't know what to say. Nobody had ever sent me a deathbed message. Not even my mother. And I didn't know exactly what "first chair" meant, though it was obviously important.

"That's wonderful," I said. "I'd like to hear you play."

"Oh, you will," she said. "All day, every day. I have to make the most of summer vacation, because there's never enough time when school starts."

She closed the case and held it on her knees, looking around the crescent dreamily, as if she weren't really seeing any of it. She didn't ask, but I told her about our family anyway — that our mom is dead, and we move a lot, and I really like where we are now.

It was hard to stop talking, but when I did, she told us about *her* family. Her father sells cars. Mostly he's very successful, but business has been bad lately, so he had to sell their house and look for a cheap place to live until he gets on his feet again. Her mother cried a lot when their beautiful house was sold, but now she has a job in a dress shop, and she says she'll be far too exhausted at the end of the day to care what they live in.

"I honestly don't see why you like it here so much," April said. She looked at me curiously, as if she were actually seeing me for the first time.

I tried to think of a good reason. I liked the way our houses clustered together, like one of those painted-plaster villages people put up at Christmastime. . . . I liked the way the woods wrapped around us, kept us safe. . . . If I told her my reasons, I was sure she'd laugh.

"I don't know exactly," I said at last. "I just think it's neat."

"Except for the moonlight —" Allie began, but right then Mrs. Danner started calling, "April! April! Come here!" She sounded frantic.

April stood up slowly and brushed off the seat of her shorts. Then she bent down and patted Sammy's head, as if she'd heard her mother call like that a million times and knew there was no hurry. "See you," she said and strode off with her violin.

When we were alone, Allie gave a deep sigh. She was thinking very hard about our conversation and so was I.

"I never knew anyone called April before," she said.

"It's a beautiful name," I said. "It fits her."

"I bet she's going to be your best friend," she went on. "Better than me."

22

That's my little sister — always right to the point. "No one could be a better friend than Allison Joslin," I assured her. "Ask Sammy if you don't believe me. Besides," I said, trying to act as if it didn't matter, "I think maybe her best friend is in that violin case."

FOUR

The Danners have been our neighbors for three days now, but until this afternoon the house might as well have still been empty. Except for the violin music, of course. April practices for hours! I never knew musicians had to work so hard.

Sometimes she plays the same few notes over and over again, trying to improve a phrase that sounded fine to me in the first place. Other times, she plays a whole piece, and it's so beautiful that I hold my breath. Dad says there's nothing better than a good violinist and nothing worse than a bad one, so we should count our blessings. Still, I wished she'd take a break once in a while. Yesterday Allie wanted to invite her to go to the playground with us, but I knew that was a bad idea. April Danner doesn't give two hoots about playgrounds.

She did stop playing this afternoon, but not because she wanted some fun. Allie was watching a soap opera, and I was on the back steps letting the sun dry my hair, when the music broke off with a kind of squawk. A moment later, April came flying out her back door. Her face was pale, and she kept looking over her shoulder as she ran.

"Somebody's in our house!" she gasped. "In the basement. Crying!"

My stomach turned over. "Couldn't be," I said. And then, when she scowled at me, "Are you sure?"

"I'm sure!" she snapped. "I don't know how she got in without my seeing her, but she's down there now."

"She?" I repeated.

"Yes, she." April pulled me to my feet. "Come on. Listen for yourself!"

It was the last thing I wanted to do. I think I *knew* right then that no one had sneaked past her while she was practicing, and I didn't want to consider the possibility of *another* haunted house. Still, this was April, my maybe someday best friend, and she needed me. At least, she needed someone, and I was glad to be that person.

"Allie," I yelled, "I'm going next door for a few minutes, okay?"

"Okay." She sounded far away. Dad doesn't like her to watch the soaps, but she loves them. I keep hoping she doesn't understand what she's seeing.

The Danners' back porch is exactly like ours, but the resemblance ends inside the door. Our furniture is sort of battered-looking and there isn't much of it. In the Danners' house, unopened packing boxes were everywhere, crammed between gleaming tables and chairs and tall, glass-fronted cabinets. I stood in the kitchen, peering in at all that beautiful clutter, admiring the Oriental rug that covered the floor in the living room. April's music stand was set squarely in the center of the rug. Sheets of music were scattered around the room.

The house was very still. "Are you sure —" I whispered.

She put her finger to her lips. "Wait," she said.

Then I heard it — a soft sobbing that drifted up the basement steps like another kind of music. It was such a sad sound that for a moment I forgot to be scared.

"I told you so!" April hissed. "I'm going to call the police."

"No, don't!" The words jumped out of my mouth. "She sounds as if she's in trouble — maybe we can talk to her. If the police come, everyone will get hyper."

You have to understand that by "everyone" I meant Dad, who hates what he calls "scenes." But my warning seemed to mean something to April, too. She put down the phone. "You're right. My mother will *die* if she finds out someone broke in here," she groaned. "She's still in a state because we had to move."

The crying continued. "Maybe it isn't a person," I said. "It could be a leaky pipe."

April didn't even bother to answer. "What can we do?" she demanded. "It might be a crazy person with a gun who sneaked in."

I shuddered and said I didn't think so. "There've been weird things happening in our house, too," I told her.

"Like what?" Before I could answer, the crying got louder, more desperate. April slumped into a chair, as if her knees wouldn't hold her up any longer. She looked at the phone again, and I knew I had to do something fast.

I opened the basement door and switched on the

light. Then I started down the steps, hoping the crying would stop now that the light was on. It didn't. When I reached the fifth step, I crouched and peered into the basement.

It didn't seem as big as ours, but I supposed that was because it was so crowded. There was lots of furniture, draped in sheets, and there were tall stacks of boxes waiting to be unpacked.

"Where is she?" April whispered from the top of the stairs.

I shrugged. The crying seemed to come from the far end of the room, but if someone was there she had plenty of places in which to hide. Just the thought of making my way between all those spooky white shapes made me want to turn around and run.

"Who's there?" I croaked. "What's wrong?"

The sobbing grew louder still. I heard April start down the stairs behind me, and I thought, It's about time! After all, it was *her* ghost. She crouched at my side, and for a few seconds neither of us moved or even breathed. Then a strange thing happened. The sobbing stayed just as intense, but it began to get softer, like the sound being turned down on a radio.

That was a whole lot scarier than if it had stopped all at once. If a real person were crying in the basement, and she was startled when I called out, wouldn't she have stopped in the middle of a sob? How could the crying of a real person just fade away?

I looked at April and knew she was thinking the same thing. She gave a choky little gasp and jumped up. We stumbled over each other's feet as we raced up the stairs and out onto the back porch. April kept going, and I followed her to the shade of the big trees at the end of the yard. We collapsed on the grass.

"What did you mean about weird things happening in your house?" April gasped when she'd caught her breath. "Is someone crying there, too?"

I told her about the footsteps I heard when I was alone, the whistling, and the disappearing picture on Allie's bedroom wall. When I got to the moonlight man and his dog, she rolled over on her stomach and shook her head.

"That's enough!" she exclaimed. "Don't tell my parents any of that stuff. You'll spoil everything!"

I held my temper. People can sound rude when they're just scared.

"How can you *not* want to know what's going on?" I asked. "You heard the crying. It was real! Maybe if we work together, we can figure out what's happening."

April shook her head impatiently. "It could all be a trick, couldn't it? Someone could have left a tape down in our basement — oh, I don't know!" She sighed. "This whole year has been a mess! My father's in a horrible mood, always talking about needing to earn more money, and my mother's a nervous wreck. They fought about moving and about her job and every little thing. If she thinks this house is haunted, she'll fall apart all over again!"

"Well, my dad's sort of the same way," I told her. "I don't mean he's nervous, but if there's even a *little* problem he'll decide we'd be better off somewhere else. And we wouldn't be. I love it here!"

For a couple of minutes we just sat staring at our houses. Then April said, "Will you do me a favor?"

That made me feel good. Sharing problems. Doing favors. Hanging out together. Being friends. It was what I'd been hoping for. "Sure," I said. "Do you want to come over and watch TV till your folks come home?"

"No, I want to go back inside and get my violin and my music," she said. "But I don't want to do it alone. I have a lesson tomorrow and I'm not ready for it."

We walked across the yard to her now-quiet house, and I waited while she gathered up her music and violin. She handed me her music stand.

"Thanks," she said when we were back at the end of the yard. "See you later."

I was being sent home! If you think my feelings were hurt, you've got it right. But since then I've been thinking about our strange conversation, and I understand what April was telling me.

Her parents' fights, the move to the crescent, hearing a ghost in her basement — talking to me! — were all just roadblocks on her way to a great violin lesson.

I wonder what it's like to be so good at something that nothing else matters.

FIVE

Allie has a boyfriend. His name is Justin and he's quite old — at least eight. She told us all about him at dinner last night. He chases her around the school playground and calls her Skinny, and sometimes they get on a teeter-totter and he bounces her really hard. Dad said it sounded like true love for sure, and Allie said no, but her face got very pink. She wanted to go back to the playground first thing this morning.

We were walking up to the path, when the Danners' back door burst open and April rushed out.

For a moment, I wondered if she wanted to come with us — silly me — but then I saw her expression. I hoped she wasn't going to talk about the crying woman in front of Allie.

"Those people!" she exclaimed. "I could kill them!"

"What people?"

She glared across our yard. "Those — those Carmeeks!"

"Carpeks," I told her. "What did they do?"

"They complained about the *noise*! She called my father and said her husband couldn't take his *nap* yesterday because I was making so much *noise* in the backyard. She wanted to know why I couldn't practice in the *house* like a *normal* person would." She was so furious that the words just popped out of her. "And so then, of course, my father wanted to know *why* I was playing outside, and my mother said if there was one thing she couldn't *bear* it was difficult neighbors, and after that they argued all evening."

"You're pretty tan, anyway," Allie said cheerfully. April stared at her, confused by the change of subject.

"I told Allie you were practicing outside because you wanted to get some sun," I said. "But if you don't want to stay in your house all day, you can practice at ours. We'll keep the windows closed so the Carpeks can't hear." Allie grabbed my hand and gave it a tug. "We're going to the playground now, but we'll be home before lunch. . . ."

April looked back at her house and bit her lip. "I don't know how you stand it," she said in a low voice. "All that stuff you told me —"

I gave Allie a little push toward the path. "You go ahead," I told her. "Justin's probably looking for you. I'll be there in a minute."

She darted off, and I tried to think of a way to explain my feelings. "I *am* afraid," I said finally. "But I want to live here more than you do, I guess."

April looked grim. "That's for sure!" she said, as she started back toward her house. "She'd just better leave me alone," she said tersely, and I wondered whether she meant Mrs. Carpek or the crying woman.

When I reached the playground, Allie was playing tag with two other girls and Justin. I settled down under a tree at the edge of the baseball diamond and opened the book I'd brought along. The air was silky-soft, and the sun was warm, not hot. I'd have at least ten new freckles before the morning was over, but I didn't care. I was glad to be there, and Allie sounded more carefree than she had for a long time.

When we went home for lunch, Mr. Carpek was in

his backyard planting petunias. He didn't look up. Allie had been chattering — Justin always chases her first when he's "It" — but she stopped talking when she saw that hunched figure so obviously determined not to know we were there. April's house was silent, but she started playing again while we ate our bologna sandwiches, and she kept at it all afternoon. If the crying woman had returned, she was being ignored.

Maybe, I thought, the haunting was over. I hadn't heard the footsteps in the upstairs hall for a couple of days, and I hadn't seen the moonlight man either, though I watched for him every evening from the kitchen windows. If you didn't act afraid of a ghost, would he — or she — give up and go away? It was a comforting thought, and I managed to hang on to it all afternoon. Tonight, though, that neat idea was shot to pieces.

I was standing at the sink, stacking the last of the dishes to dry, when I saw a movement at the end of the yard. Dad was still in the kitchen, scooping a handful of peanuts from a jar, and I almost called him to come and look. If it had been a real prowler, I would have, but then the figure separated itself from the darkness of the woods behind it and I saw that it was the moonlight man. His little dog was behind him. They stopped and faced our house, so that it seemed as if we must be staring at each other. Then they moved on, with that weird kind of gliding movement, until they were opposite the Danners' house. They stopped there. I hoped Mrs. Danner wasn't looking out. She'd be packed up and ready to leave by tomorrow morning!

After a while, the two shapes — one tall and thin, one small and stubby — began to fade. By the time they were gone completely, the television was on in our living room, and Dad and Allie were watching a sitcom. I went in and sat on the couch beside them. My heart was thudding so loudly, it seemed as if they would have to notice.

What I would have liked to do right then was hug them both and tell them how much I loved them. I wanted to tell them I was going to keep them safe and happy, no matter what. Instead, I just sat there, laughing when they did, till the show was over and it was time for Allie to go to bed. She wanted to stay up awhile longer, but Dad said no.

"Sorry you have to play mother so much," he said when we were alone. "It's not fair."

"That's okay," I told him quickly. "I like it."

"Want me to go up and tuck her in tonight?"

I was going to say Allie would really like that, but then she called from upstairs.

"Jenneee!" There was a little quiver in her voice that had me on my feet in a flash. "I'll go," I said over my shoulder and practically ran up the stairs.

She was crouched on the edge of her bed, her eyes huge and staring. The Peter Pan poster we'd taped next to the back window lay facedown on the floor.

"Don't look so scared," I told her. "The curtain must have blown against it. We'll put it up again tomorrow."

She shivered. "The picture was there," she said in a small voice. "When I came in it was there, just like the other time — the boys in the old car without a top. It was there!"

I sat down next to her and took a steadying breath. "I think you're pretty tired," I said. "When people are tired they sometimes imagine things."

We sat for a moment, staring at the dark rectangle on the wallpaper, and then she stood up and began pulling off her clothes.

"Stay here till I fall asleep, okay?" she said softly.

I said I would. "You can sleep with me if you want to," I told her. "Or we can trade rooms." I hated for her to be afraid.

She shook her head and ran across the hall to the bathroom. When she came back she jumped into bed and pulled the sheet up to her nose.

"I want this room," she said from under the sheet. "I can see the squirrel's nest and the woods and the whole backyard from my window. I don't want to trade." And then she added something wonderful.

"Don't tell Daddy about the picture," she said. "Don't tell him I was scared. We want him to like it here."

Six

It's been three days since Allie last saw the picture. The next morning I put up the poster again, using tacks this time. Then we went down to the basement and opened a couple of cartons that hadn't been unpacked in our last apartment. Mom's embroidered tablecloth was in one, and when we spread it on the table, I remembered long-ago Sunday dinners, with company filling up our dining room and the smell of roasting chicken in the air. I smoothed the tablecloth and imagined Mom humming in the kitchen as she filled bowls with good things to eat.

The other box held some fancy dishes. There was a

set of four fruit plates that we decided to hang on the dining room wall — or rather, I decided. Allie got pretty bored with the measuring and pounding, but when the plates were in place she was polite and pretended not to notice that one was a little lower than the rest.

Dad didn't comment when we sat down to eat that night — maybe seeing the tablecloth made him sad — but the next evening he brought home a big bouquet of Queen Anne's lace he'd picked in a field along the highway.

"Looks nice," he said, when I put the flowers in a china vase and set it on the table. "Looks like home."

Since then I've hung more pictures, and yesterday morning I painted Allie's dresser yellow. Kathy Burton gave me the paint, left over from their kitchen cabinets. It's very bright, and Allie loves it.

The way I look at it, each thing I do makes this house a little more ours. When three days pass without a problem, I feel as if I'm winning some secret war!

Then last night April came over after dinner. I knew as soon as I saw her that if the day had been another happy one for me, for her it had been something else.

"*She* was down there again this afternoon," she said in a low voice.

"The crying woman?"

"Who else?"

"What did you do?"

Her eyes sparked. "I kept on playing. Actually, it was sort of a relief when I finally heard her. I'd been expecting it every minute. It's been awful — I can't concentrate on anything important."

I didn't know what to say.

"I was thinking maybe — maybe if we can figure out what's going on. . . ." She looked at me anxiously. "You want to, don't you? You said weird things happen in your house, too."

I nodded. This time she had said *we*. We would work together.

"It must have something to do with the people who used to live in our two houses," I said. "We can try to find out about that. The Carpeks probably know — they've lived here forever."

"Well, I'm certainly not going to talk to *them*," April snapped. "After the mean things they said about my music!"

"I'll ask," I offered. And then I took a chance. "But you have to come with me."

41

I thought she was going to say no. I could tell she wanted to, even if it meant listening to the crying woman for the rest of the summer. Then she shrugged.

"Okay," she agreed. "But if they say one word about my *noise* —"

"I'll tell them I'm going to take drum lessons." She glared at me for a moment and then realized it was a joke.

"We'll do it tomorrow morning," I promised. "First I'll go with Allie to the playground. She knows some of the kids now, so she can stay there by herself for a while."

When I went to bed last night I could hardly wait for morning to come.

April was waiting when I came back from the playground the next morning.

"That old man's gone out," she reported. "He walked down the road about five minutes ago wearing his goofy red baseball cap."

"Good!" I said. One Carpek was plenty.

The television was playing when we went next door, and I had to ring the bell a couple of times before Mrs. Carpek came. She's small and wispy-looking, with thick glasses and short, straight gray hair. When she saw who was on the porch, she took a step backward.

"What do you want? My husband isn't home."

I said we'd like to talk to her for a few minutes. "I don't want to buy anything," she said. "I'm very busy."

April muttered under her breath. "We're not selling," I said. "We just want to talk."

Mrs. Carpek tightened her lips as if to make it clear *she* wasn't going to say a word, but she did open the screen door then and let us in. She even turned off the sound on the television, but her expression said, "Hurry up and get this over with." She kept glancing out the living room windows — hoping to see the red baseball cap, I suppose.

"We wondered if you could tell us about the people who used to live in my house. And in April's — she lives on the other side of us."

"I know that," Mrs. Carpek snapped, and for a moment I was afraid she was going to say something mean about the violin playing. "We keep to ourselves," she announced instead. "We learned that lesson fifty years ago, and we won't forget it. If you keep to yourself, there won't be any trouble."

"Was there trouble fifty years ago?" April asked

unexpectedly. I'd thought I would have to ask all the questions.

"I don't see that it's any of your business," Mrs. Carpek retorted. She looked out the window again. "Why do you ask that? Did your parents send you over here?"

"We don't mean to be nosy," I said. "It's just —"

"Just foolishness!" Mrs. Carpek exclaimed. "I don't want to talk about it to you and I won't! If people can't control their children it's not our fault!"

I glanced at April. Was Mrs. Carpek talking about us or about people who had lived in the crescent fifty years ago? Whichever it was, she suddenly sounded as if she were about to cry.

"I've got work to do," she said, as a teakettle began to whistle out in the kitchen. "My husband's going to want coffee when he gets back." She turned and left us alone in the living room.

"Let's get out of here!" April whispered. "I don't want to be around when he gets back."

It seemed like a good idea. If Mrs. Carpek was rude to us, he would probably be a lot worse.

We were going down the front steps when Mrs. Carpek screamed. At first, I thought she might have burned herself with the teakettle, but then she cried, "Arthur, Arthur," and started sobbing.

I started back into the house.

"She doesn't want us in there," April protested. "You heard her!"

"She wants *someone*," I said and kept on going.

The old lady stood at a kitchen window, clutching the counter as if she might faint. We peered over her shoulders, and there was Mr. Carpek lying facedown at the far end of the yard. I recognized the plaid shirt and blue jeans he always wore, and the red baseball cap that lay next to him. His thin white hair moved a little in the breeze.

For a moment we just stared. Then Mrs. Carpek ran out to the back hall, and April followed her. I looked around for a telephone, thinking I ought to call for help, but then I ran, too.

What happened next was impossible, and I know it. From the time we left the window till we reached the backyard, no more than four or five seconds could have passed. And yet, when we burst through the back door, Mr. Carpek was gone! There was no sign of the body we'd seen from the kitchen window.

"Oh," Mrs. Carpek gasped and added, unbelievably, "Never mind, then."

I wondered if I'd heard right. *Never mind?*

"Maybe he crawled into the woods," April suggested, but that was impossible. No one — certainly not a frail old man — could have recovered consciousness and crawled out of sight that fast.

"I said it's all right," Mrs. Carpek repeated in a steadier voice. "I made a dumb mistake. Somebody must have dropped a bundle of clothes back there, and now they've blown away." She actually tried to smile when she said that — a painful smile that barely moved her lips.

"What's all this?" The gruff voice made us jump. April gave a little shriek as we turned and saw Mr. Carpek coming around from the front of the house. His cap was pushed to the back of his head, and his face was sweaty. He carried a net bag full of soft-drink cans.

At first no one answered. Then we all spoke at once.

"It's nothing, Arthur," Mrs. Carpek said. "A mistake."

I said, "We came to talk to you."

April said, "We thought we saw you lying back there in the grass."

Mr. Carpek looked as if he were sorting out our answers. He kept his eyes on his wife. "If it's nothing, then why stand around out here? I want my coffee." He dropped the net bag at the foot of the steps and clumped up the stairs as if April and I weren't there. Mrs. Carpek scurried inside after him.

"That was *not* a pile of clothes somebody dropped," April said shakily.

I agreed. "So what do you think it was?"

She scowled. "A ghost with a nasty sense of humor? The only thing I'm sure of is that they are really rude people! Both of them!"

I agreed with her there, too. But tonight, while I'm writing, I keep remembering the long look that passed between the Carpeks as they went inside. They may not want to talk to us, but they know a lot about what's happening in the crescent, and they are afraid.

SEVEN

This morning Dad said, "You know, you kids can ride into town with me anytime you want to. If you don't want to wait till the store closes, you can take the bus home."

I'd been thinking about that, but I'd been waiting till I had a whole list of things to do. We needed curtains for the kitchen — our last three apartments hadn't had kitchen windows. And a shower curtain — I'd seen a picture of one with bright-colored fish all over it. Dad does the actual buying, but he likes me to look around first. Usually he goes along with my choices, because he really doesn't care one way or another.

"We'll go today," I said. Yesterday my list had suddenly grown longer. Without meaning to, Mrs. Carpek had hinted that something important — some kind of trouble — had taken place in the crescent fifty years ago. I wanted to find out the names of the families who'd been living in April's house and ours in 1949.

As we wound down the road to the highway I thought about how when fall comes I'll be making that trip every day. I'll be going to another new school, starting all over *again*, with kids who've known one another forever. It'll help to know our house is waiting for me to come home. That's how I feel — as if the house wants us in it as much as I want us to be there. Don't ask me why!

Allie was excited about the day in town, especially since Justin was going somewhere with his mother and wouldn't be at the playground. Dad dropped us at the mall, and we made a quick trip through a couple of stores, looking at curtains, with a side trip in each to the toy department. Then we took a bus to Mangold Avenue and walked until we found the Kromner Real Estate Company.

The office was small and cluttered, with only one

person behind the counter. A kid-hater — I could tell that as soon as she looked up. She glared and went back to her papers.

We just stood there, waiting, until she finally looked up again. "You can sit over there if you're meeting your parents," she said, pointing at a row of straight-backed chairs.

I told her we weren't meeting anyone. We needed information about the house Mr. Kromner had rented us. When I mentioned Mr. Kromner, she put down her pencil.

"Name?"

I gave her Dad's name and our address and said that I was there to find out who had lived in the house fifty years ago. I didn't exactly *say* my father had sent me, but it sounded that way.

"I suppose you can look at the file," she said, sounding as offended as if I'd asked to look into her handbag. "Though why you should want to . . ." The words trailed off as she took a folder from a file drawer and laid it on the counter. "The deed will be on top. Don't get the papers out of order." She went back to her work.

Allie poked me. "Let's go," she whispered. "I don't like it here."

"I don't, either," I whispered back. But I was pretty pleased with myself, just the same. The history of our house was there in front of me.

I read fast and learned that some people named Tate had built our house fifty-three years ago. It had cost them four thousand dollars. Three years later they had sold it for twenty-five hundred. A Mr. Peterson bought it and lived there for thirteen years. The next owners, the Geers, stayed for fourteen years. Then the Kromner Real Estate Company bought it. I wrote all the names and dates on the back of the notes I'd made about the curtains.

"Is there any way I can get information about the Tate family?" I asked the clerk. "They sold the house just three years after they built it."

She sighed impatiently and turned the folder around to look at the deed. "Well, they weren't very smart about selling property, obviously," she sneered. "Other than that —" She put the deed to one side and flipped through the letters in the file. After a moment, she pushed one of them across the counter. It was addressed to the Kromner Real Estate Company, asking them to sell the house as quickly as possible since the family was moving. The letter was signed "Edgar Tate."

"Do you think I could look at the deed of the house next door to ours?" I asked cautiously. "Just for a minute? The one the Danners are renting."

She looked shocked. "Certainly not!" She shut the folder with a snap. "Mr. Kromner wouldn't want you looking into someone else's private papers."

Allie had been leaning against me, but now she straightened and started for the door. I said, "Thanks, anyway," and hurried after her.

We walked to the corner without speaking. Then Allie said, "I'm not going back there, ever."

"Neither am I," I told her. If I want to learn the names of the Tates' neighbors, I'll find another way, I thought.

Still, the visit had been worth the trouble. We had the answer to one question — who owned our house fifty years ago — *and* we'd uncovered a mystery!

Why had the Tates been willing to sell their almost-new house for just a little over half of what they'd paid for it? Why had they moved?

We had lunch — cheeseburgers and chocolate shakes — at Hamburger Heaven. By the time we'd finished, Allie was smiling again, and I had planned our next move.

"We're going to the library," I told her. "You can

take out as many books as you want. I have something to look up."

"What?" She looked at me suspiciously. "Will it take a long time?"

"Just a few minutes — you'll see." I knew that once she started wandering up and down between the bookshelves in the children's department, it wouldn't matter how slow I was. "I'm going to look through some old newspapers on microfilm. We learned how in school last year."

I waited for her to ask what I was going to look for, but she didn't. "Old newspapers" probably sounded dull.

A few minutes later I was settled in front of a screen with microfilm of the *Newton Herald* for 1949. I knew there were lots of reasons why the Tates might have left the crescent in a hurry. Maybe Mr. Tate lost his job. Or maybe — and this was what I hoped to find out — something had happened that made it necessary for him to go away. I skimmed the headlines, looking for the name Tate, not sure what I expected to find.

An hour later I gave up. If the Tates were in trouble in 1949, it wasn't the kind that was reported in a newspaper.

I returned the films, picked out three mysteries for myself, and went to find Allie. She was curled up in a window seat with a whole stack of books beside her.

"That's too many," I told her. "I know I said you could take all you wanted, but they won't let you have that many."

"I've already checked them out," she said. "I can carry them." She started stacking the books carefully in the curve of her arm. When the pile reached her chin, I gave in and took half of them.

"Don't forget, we have to walk from the bus stop all the way up to the crescent," I warned her. "And it looks like rain."

By the time we got on the bus, we were tired and sticky, and I was discouraged besides. If I couldn't find anything about the Tates in the *Herald*, and the Carpeks wouldn't talk to me, I didn't know what to do next.

The sky got grayer as we rolled across town, and when we got out at Crescent Lane, the woods looked dark and unfriendly.

"We can wait here till Daddy comes home and picks us up," Allie said. "We can read."

"And get soaked," I said. "No, thank you." I started to walk and she trailed after me, shifting books from one arm to the other.

"We're not supposed to walk in the woods," she said after a couple of minutes. "We might get lost."

"We're not walking *in* the woods, we're walking *through* them," I said. I hardly ever get annoyed with Allie, but I was tired and disappointed, and the books were heavy. "Dad told us to take the bus, remember? He knew we'd have to walk up the hill."

"My arms ache," she said after we'd gone around another curve.

"Think about something else," I told her. "Listen to the birds." But that turned out to be the wrong thing to say. The words were no sooner out of my mouth than the birds stopped singing.

EIGHT

It's a little thing — hearing birds sing — but when they stop, the silence is *huge*.

"What happened?" Allie whispered. Her eyes were very wide, and I was suddenly aware of how alone we were. Dad and Mike Burton wouldn't be coming up the road for at least forty-five minutes. Unless a delivery-man happened along, or the Carpeks, we were on our own.

"Something must have scared the birds — an owl, maybe," I told her. "Just keep walking. One more curve and we're there — I think."

Without discussing it, we moved to the center of

the road. I guess we half-expected something horrible to burst out of the woods in front of us. What appeared was a dog, a small black-and-white terrier, and it didn't burst out. It sort of waddled.

At the edge of the blacktop the dog sat down and looked over its shoulder as if it were waiting for someone. We passed it, making a wide loop to the far side of the road. Then a soft whistling began, deep in the woods.

I gave Allie a little push and said, "Walk faster. It's going to rain." She glanced up at me, and I knew she wasn't fooled.

When I looked back, the dog was still there, staring at nothing. Then we rounded the last curve and the crescent was in front of us, wonderfully safe and *ordinary*. I could hear April's violin and the sound of clapping that must have come from the Carpeks' television. Allie began to run, scattering books behind her. I gathered them up, and we both stumbled up our porch steps and into the house.

"That was the moonlight dog," Allie said when she'd curled up in a corner of the sofa. She was one beat away from sucking her thumb.

I said, "You don't know that."

"And that was the moonlight man whistling," she went on. "Do you think he can whistle?"

I shrugged. I wasn't going to tell her I'd heard that whistle before — the same tune! — right here in our house.

After dinner I went next door to tell April about our day. After all, she'd wanted me to see what I could find out. But she acted tired, and I wondered if her mother and father had kept her awake arguing about the house. The dog in the road didn't impress her at all. Why shouldn't a person walk with his dog in the woods if he wanted to? She was more interested when I described my detective work at the real-estate office and the library.

"But you still don't know anything important," she decided glumly when I'd finished. "And you don't know what to do next, do you?"

I asked if she'd heard the crying woman again, and she said no, but she kept expecting to, and that was just as bad. We talked about other things — the cranky clerk at the real-estate office, the curtains I'd picked out — but I could tell none of that interested her.

"How about going over to the Burtons'?" I said. "They're fun."

She shook her head, so I said good night and went

by myself. April and I aren't going to solve the mystery together after all. I understood that, once and for all, as I walked around the crescent. She doesn't care why our houses are haunted; she just wants it to stop. I want it to stop, too, but the *why* is important.

The Burtons were on their knees pulling weeds from the bed of geraniums and marigolds that edged their porch. The red and gold flowers were bright and happy-looking, like everything else in that house. The weeds looked pretty healthy, too.

"We plant and we forget," Kathy said cheerfully. "That's our trouble. But we decided if it rains tonight, the weeds will be bigger than the geraniums by morning." She stood up and brushed dirt off her knees. "Let's have some lemonade. We need a break."

"Good idea," Mike said. I thought, Whatever she says will always sound like a good idea to him. We sat on the front steps, sipping lemonade and watching the sky grow dark.

"What have you been up to?" Kathy asked. "Besides painting your cute little sister's bureau?"

I told them, leaving out the scary walk home and the real reason why I went to Mr. Kromner's office. "I wanted to know everything about our house," I said, which was the truth, sort of.

"Good for you," Mike said. "Go straight to the source. My boss would be impressed."

"Your boss?" I didn't know where he worked.

"The city editor at the *Herald*," he said. "I'm the smallest fish in the newsroom pond."

I was thrilled. I'd never known a newspaper reporter before.

"Kathy's assistant to the advertising manager," he went on proudly. "Between us we make almost enough to afford the payments on this house."

"We met at the drinking fountain and got engaged in the cafeteria," Kathy added, giggling.

"And lived happily ever after," Mike said, but he didn't laugh.

"So what did you find out about your house?" Kathy asked.

I told her I had the names of all the people who had owned it, and that was all. "The people who built it were called Tate, but they sold it after just three years — I don't know why."

"You could ask the Carpeks," Kathy said. "They'll know."

I said I'd tried that. "They don't want to talk about the people who used to live here. Mrs. Carpek didn't even want to let us in. She says they like to keep to themselves."

Mike chuckled. "Except sometimes," he said. "Would you believe they called Kromner to complain about the color we were painting our wall? They didn't know we'd bought the place and can do what we want with it. I think they're worried about what color we'll choose for the outside."

"We're thinking of purple with bright green shutters," Kathy said, so solemnly that it took me a moment to see she was joking. "Actually, I feel sorry for those poor old souls. I've never seen either one of them smile, have you?"

I wonder what the Burtons would say if I told them what happened when we visited the Carpeks. *April and I saw Mr. Carpek lying in the backyard and Mrs. Carpek started screaming and then he just disappeared. . . .* It sounds crazy, even to me.

Someday I'd like to tell them everything that's happened since we moved here, but I couldn't do it today. We're friends. They treat me almost like a grown-up. I don't want them to decide I'm just a silly kid after all, with a wild imagination.

NINE

At first the bright lights were part of my dream. I was in a little boat — it was about as long as a bathtub! — and I was trying to reach an island. There was lightning all around me, and the waves were as big as hills. No matter how hard I rowed, the island kept getting farther away.

When I woke up, the brightness was still there. Blue-and-white bursts of light filled the bedroom. After a few seconds I realized the bursts were too regular to be lightning. I ran to the window and looked out.

My bedroom is the front one, so I have a good view

of the crescent. A squad car, its lights flashing, stood in front of the Danners' house. The passenger door was open, and I could hear crackly voices on the radio. Next door, all the lights were on. As I watched, Dad went down our front steps and crossed to the Danners' porch. He knocked, and when no one answered he went in anyway.

I tiptoed down the hall and peeked at Allie. She was sound asleep, with Sammy cuddled under her chin. Then I went back to my window and leaned against the screen, wondering what was going on. It would be terrible if April's mother or father had had a heart attack, or if a burglar had heard about all their beautiful things and had broken in. But even as I turned over the possibilities, I think I guessed the truth about what had brought the police to the crescent. When Dad came home ten minutes later, his old slippers flip-flopping across the lawn, I found out I was right.

"They thought they heard someone crying in the basement!" He chuckled. "Both Mr. and Mrs. Danner — can you believe that? He went downstairs to look around, and then his wife called the police."

"What about April?" I asked.

"Sleeping," he said. "Says she didn't hear a thing. Acts as if her parents are out of their minds — which

63

her mother may well be, if you ask me. You never heard such a fuss!" He shook his head. "Danner's pretty embarrassed. The police searched the whole basement — there's a mountain of stuff down there — and they didn't see or hear a thing."

We crowded close to the window as the voices outside grew louder. Two policemen had come out of the house with Mr. Danner, in his bathrobe, trailing behind them. We heard him say he was very sorry his wife had called them and she wouldn't bother them again.

"Where does *he* think the crying came from?" I asked curiously.

Dad grinned. "He says it must have been air in the pipes — these are old houses. Or a shutter squeaking in the wind, or . . ."

"No wind," I reminded him.

He cocked his head at me. "Well, then, I suppose Mrs. Danner is right — the house is haunted," he said dryly. "Whatever! If you ask me, they're both capable of imagining the whole thing. The girl — your friend — is the most levelheaded one in that bunch."

He might not have been quite so sure if he'd been home when April came over this morning. She had blue shadows under her eyes, and her mouth was set in a tight line.

"I guess you know about last night," she said.

I nodded. "Allie slept through the whole thing. She's outside, but if she comes in we have to stop talking about it."

"That's fine with me," April said bitterly. "I wish I never had to talk about it or think about it again. My mother didn't go to sleep for hours, she was so scared. And my father was no help — he acted as if the crying was her fault. That's not all." She went to the kitchen window to watch for Allie. "I was lying in bed listening to them and thinking what a mess everything is, and all of a sudden something hit the screen on my bedroom window. Pebbles, I think."

"Pebbles!"

"It happened twice. When I looked out, no one was there. At least I couldn't see anyone, but I felt as if someone was looking up at me. I'm practically sure of it." She nibbled a fingernail. "If I had mentioned *that* to my father this morning, he would have absolutely blown up. He told my mother he doesn't want to hear any more nonsense about ghosts." She pulled out a kitchen chair and plunked down. "Oh, I hate this!"

"I don't blame you for being frightened," I began, but that was as far as I got.

"I'm not just *frightened*," she interrupted, as if I'd said something silly. "This is the most important time in my whole entire life. My violin teacher says if I work hard all summer I'll be ready to do more advanced work this fall. There's a teacher in Chicago who takes one scholarship student a year. His name is Jacob Mindler. Mr. Cargio wants me to audition in September."

I said, "That's wonderful!" and her lips twisted.

"It's not wonderful if I can't practice!" she snapped. "Between your ghosts and my folks' arguing, I'm not half ready for my lesson today."

"They're not *my* ghosts," I told her. I was annoyed and impressed at the same time. "Listen," I said, "why don't you practice here? We'll close the windows so the Carpeks can't complain, and Allie and I will stay out of your way." I was trying hard to cheer her up. "And when you go to town for your lesson, we'll go, too. I'll look through the old *Herald*s again, but this time I'll go slower and concentrate on fifty years ago this summer. Maybe I missed something important."

"What's the use?" April said gloomily. But after a few more heavy sighs she went home to get her violin, and when Allie and I left for the playground she was already hard at work. I wondered if I should remind her about the footsteps and whistling in the upstairs hall. Better not, I decided. I hadn't heard anything for a few days.

When we came home two hours later, she looked a little less uptight. I made bologna sandwiches, and then Allie and I went upstairs for another hour so April could practice some more. At two-thirty Mrs. Danner came home from work to take April to her lesson on the other side of Newton. She smiled sort of weakly when we all got into the car, but she didn't talk to us at all. It was a relief to get out at the library.

I hadn't said anything to April, but her story about pebbles thrown at the window had given me an idea. Maybe the moonlight man and the crying woman were connected in some way. If that was true, then I was probably wasting my time looking at crime reports. I checked out the *Herald* microfilms for May, June, July, and August of 1949 and turned to the society pages. Allie sat with me this time and watched curiously as columns of engagement notices flicked across the screen.

"Watch for Tate," I told her. "It might be a man's

name or a woman's. People named Tate used to live in our house a long time ago."

"How do you know?"

"That's what I found out at the real-estate office, where that sweet lady helped us." I made a face, and Allie giggled.

"But why does it matter?"

"It doesn't," I said. "I'm just nosy."

We went through the May and June issues pretty fast without finding a Tate. By the time we reached July, Allie had made two trips to the watercooler and I was getting bored myself. Engagement notices are dull reading — just names and dates. That was probably why my eyes wandered to a news item tucked in at the bottom of one page. The headline said THEFT AT TRANS-UNION, and it reported a burglary at the Trans-Union Trucking Company. Several leads were being followed up "according to Newton Police Dept. Lt. Arthur Carpek."

"What's the matter?" Allie asked. "Why did you stop? Did you find Tate?"

"No." I pointed to Carpek and waited while she spelled it out. "I think that's our neighbor," I said. "Arthur Carpek. It says here he was a policeman."

Allie looked at me. "He couldn't be," she said. "He's old."

"He wasn't fifty years ago."

But I knew what she meant. It's practically impossible to imagine that shuffling, bad-tempered old man as a sturdy young policeman, tracking down criminals.

TEN

"If it's bad news, I'm not going to listen," April said in a low voice. "I've just had the worst lesson of my entire life. Mr. Cargio actually asked if I was sick!"

April's mother had parked the car next to the house and gone inside without saying good-bye, and Allie had wandered off on business of her own. I know she was as relieved as I was to reach the end of the long, silent ride home.

I told April about finding Mr. Carpek's name in a news story, and she shrugged.

"So he was a policeman once," she said. "I don't see what that's got to do with anything. All he does now is complain about noise and make noise himself." She glared across our yards at the Carpeks' house. The old man was up on the roof, hammering fiercely and muttering loudly enough for us to hear.

I'd been thinking about him all the way home, and I'd come up with a theory. I was about to explain it, when there was a *thud*, followed by a roar of anger. Mr. Carpek had dropped his hammer. It slid down the roof and tumbled to the ground.

"Serves him right," April muttered and started up her porch steps.

I watched Mr. Carpek. He was trying to get to the ladder that was propped near the corner of the house, but reaching for the hammer had thrown him off balance. He looked like a skinny spider flattened against the shingles.

"Listen to him!" April hissed. "He knows every four-letter word there is!"

I could hardly believe what happened next. As Mr. Carpek peered over his shoulder and groped with his left foot, the ladder sort of shuddered. Then it slid sideways and crashed to the ground. He hadn't touched it.

At first, we were too startled to move, but when Mr. Carpek yelled, I started to run, and April came after me.

"Hang on!" I shouted — as if he needed anyone to tell him that! The ladder was heavy and hard to lift. We raised it clumsily, and the end scraped across a shutter with an ugly squeal. Then the top rung settled against the eaves, and we leaned against either side to hold it steady. Mr. Carpek scrambled down, swearing all the way.

I picked up the hammer and handed it to him.

"I want to know who was fooling around with my ladder!" he growled. "Crazy kids! I might have been killed!"

I couldn't believe he was accusing us, but he was.

"We weren't anywhere near your stupid ladder," April said, just as snarly. "You probably kicked it yourself."

"I didn't!"

"No, you didn't," I told him. "It fell by itself."

"Couldn't have," he said. But I think he knew I was telling the truth. He looked up at the ladder, and his lined, red face turned a little pale. Then he noticed the scratch on his shutter.

"You'd better be glad I have some brown paint left," he grumped. "You sure made a mess."

I grabbed April's arm and dragged her away before she could give him a lecture on being grateful.

"I bet he's going to call my father and complain about our saving his life!" she said furiously. "Of all the mean —"

"Mean, but scared, too," I interrupted. "Couldn't you tell? He knows someone or something's trying to hurt him. Remember how Mrs. Carpek panicked when we thought we saw him lying in the grass — and then she wanted us to forget it? And now a ladder falls over as he's about to step on it, and he doesn't want to talk about that, either. There've probably been other scary things, too. It all fits in with my theory!"

"What theory?" April shot another black look over her shoulder, but Mr. Carpek was no longer around to notice. I guess he'd had enough climbing for one day.

"Ever since I saw Mr. Carpek's name in the *Herald* I've been thinking about it," I told her. "Our houses are haunted, but I don't think anyone's tried to scare us — not yet, at least. It's the Carpeks who are in trouble. And I'll bet it has something to do with the reason the Tates sold their house fifty years ago. They'd only lived in it for three years, and they sold it for about half of what it cost them. I bet there was a huge fight. . . . Mr. Tate couldn't stand living here anymore . . . maybe —"

"You're making all that up," April said flatly. "And even if you're right, that doesn't explain why *our* house is haunted. The only thing I'm sure of is that we never should have moved here!" She ran up her porch steps, and this time she kept on going. The screen door slammed behind her.

ELEVEN

I was standing in front of the Danners' house, wondering what to do with my theory, when Mike and Kathy drove into the crescent in their rattly old sedan. Mike blew the horn, Kathy waved, and before I knew it I was following them down their driveway to the garage.

I still didn't want to tell them about the ghosts, but I had to talk to someone. Mr. Carpek's ladder had seemed like a signal to me. There was real danger in our peaceful-looking neighborhood. If I wanted our family to stay there — and I did, more than anything! — I was going to need help.

"Come on in and talk while I fix supper," Kathy said. "Mike can get us some cheese and crackers."

I was supposed to be starting dinner myself, but I went anyway. The Burtons were my friends.

Kathy took a head of lettuce from the refrigerator and handed it to me. "You can start the salad," she said, "while you tell us what's new on the home front. Have you talked to our jolly neighbors the Carpeks about the people who used to live in your house?"

"Sort of," I told her. "But I didn't find out much." I took a deep breath. "Something really strange happened while April and I were talking to Mrs. Carpek."

I described our conversation and then what we'd seen in the backyard. "It was Mr. Carpek lying out there — you would have thought so, too, if you'd been there. He was wearing a plaid shirt and that red baseball cap. But when we ran out to help him, he was gone. And a couple of minutes later he came around the side of the house, and he was perfectly all right." I kept my eyes on the lettuce I was tearing to bits. "He didn't know what we were talking about."

I waited, but the Burtons didn't say anything.

"There's a lot more you don't know about," I went on, before I lost my nerve. I described the moonlight man and his dog, the picture that kept reappearing in Allie's room, the footsteps, the whistling, and the crying woman in the Danners' basement. I told about finding Lt. Carpek's name in a fifty-year-old *Herald*.

"And today," I finished up, "just before you came home, Mr. Carpek's ladder fell over just as he was going to climb down from his roof. April and I saw it happen. He could have been killed."

Still no one spoke. I dried the lettuce in a clean towel Kathy had laid on the counter. When I finally turned around, she was shaking her head, and Mike was staring at the vinyl floor as if he'd never noticed it before.

"We knew something was going on," Kathy said. Her voice was funny-gentle, as if she were talking to a sick person. "You've looked so worried, Jenny. I can see why, if you really believe all this."

"Well, sure I believe it," I said, more sharply than I'd intended. "I didn't make it up. I just don't know what to do about it."

"How about searching for reasonable explanations?" Kathy said. "Once you start thinking in terms of ghosts, it's so easy to imagine —" She stopped and looked at Mike.

"You're the hardheaded one in this family," he told her. "But I think Jenny's pretty hardheaded, too. So if she says she's seen a ghost —" he cocked his head at me — "it's all right with me. I've always wanted to meet a ghost myself. Now it sounds as if we may have a whole bunch of them here in the neighborhood — male, female, and canine, too. What an opportunity!"

I emptied the lettuce into a bowl and dried my hands. "I have to go home and check on Allie," I said, sounding so stiff and prissy that I hated myself. "Thanks for listening. I don't blame you for laughing."

"Who's laughing?" Mike said quickly. "We just don't like to see you unhappy. Listen, I might be able to get some more information about the Tates for you. We have files at the paper — facts that might never have gotten into print. I'll look up Carpek, too," he added. "Cranky old geezer! I wonder what kind of policeman he made."

I told him that would be great. Kathy hugged me and said I should come back soon, and I promised I would. But as I cut across their backyard to our house,

I was sure they were chuckling together about the moonlight man.

I should have known better than to tell them. I *do* know better. You can't make people believe. They have to see for themselves, and even then they may tell you there has to be a reasonable explanation.

TWELVE

Maybe Mike and Kathy are right. Is that what you're thinking as you read this? *This Jenny Joslin makes up a lot of crazy stuff for her journal.* Well, I'll tell you something: I couldn't have made up today — not in a million years!

It started while Allie and I were having breakfast. Dad had already left for work, and so had the Danners. A few seconds later, April was in our kitchen, carrying her violin case and a folder of music.

"Well, it happened again!" she exclaimed. Her face was flushed. "I knew it would."

Allie asked, "What happened?" and April jumped.

She hadn't noticed her sitting there behind a cereal box. I made a warning face.

"Well," April said carefully, "there's something in our basement that makes funny noises — a pipe, I guess. It woke us up again last night."

I wished Allie would go outside, but she didn't move. "Did you find out which pipe it is?" I asked.

"My father says it's in the far end of the basement. There's a boarded-up section with a little door in it. When he found the door was locked he was so mad he called Mr. Kromner in the middle of the night. You should have heard him! He said we'd rented the whole house, and we have a right to go into every part of it. He said Kromner better have the key ready for him after work tonight."

"What kind of noise does the pipe make?" Allie wanted to know.

I told her it was very loud. "That's why April would rather practice here until it gets fixed."

"Today will be the last time," April said confidently. "My father's going to get rid of it tonight. My mother's going to my aunt's house after work, and she says she's not going to come home until it's been taken care of."

Allie was wide-eyed at the thought of a mother who would leave home because of a noisy pipe. She couldn't understand what the excitement was about, but I knew now why April sounded cheerful, even triumphant. Her father was going to have to stop pretending there was nothing wrong.

"Did Mr. Kromner say what's in the boarded-up space?" I asked.

April shook her head. "He said our house is part of a trust, and the owner wanted the door kept locked. He said no one else ever made a big deal about it."

I was getting as excited as she was. "I bet there never was a problem before," I said. "That proves there's something special about this summer. What if Mr. Kromner won't give your dad the key?"

She started sorting through her music. "Oh, he has to," she said. "If he doesn't, my father will force the lock." She glanced toward the living room, and I knew she wanted to start practicing.

"Run upstairs and get your sweater," I told Allie. She hesitated, hoping to hear more, until I reminded her that Justin would be waiting at the playground.

"Listen," I said, as soon as Allie was gone, "you have to call me when your father's going to unlock that door. I want to be there."

She looked doubtful. "I'm not supposed to talk about it to you or anybody else. He's afraid people will think he believes in ghosts. You'd have to pretend you just happened to come over." She hesitated. "I don't *think* he'd tell you to go home."

I was willing to take a chance. I thought about that boarded-up space all day — at the playground with Allie, and later, on the bus to the mall. I *knew* it was going to help me solve the puzzle.

Dad had bought the kitchen curtains we'd chosen, and now he'd said we could pick out bedspreads. That was a good sign — he'd suggested the bedspreads himself. Allie wanted one with a huge yellow sun on it to match her yellow dresser, and I chose an old-fashioned quilt. I have a picture of our mother sitting on the edge of her bed when she was a girl, and there's a quilt on the bed. My grandmother probably made it.

It was nearly five o'clock when we got off the bus at the foot of Crescent Lane, so we waited there till Dad came home and picked us up. Mr. Danner's car wasn't in the driveway where he usually left it, and I was relieved. I needed time to figure out how I was going to get away from Allie for a few minutes. Usually she watched TV after dinner, but she'd been very curious about that noisy pipe. If she thought I was going over to April's house this evening, she'd want to go, too.

It was practically a miracle, the way it turned out. When we were through eating, Dad started lugging old blankets and tarps out of the basement. We'd borrowed them to cover our furniture when we moved, and he'd decided that this was the evening to take them back.

"To our old apartment?" Allie exclaimed. "I want to go with you. I want to see Jeffy and Joy Marie."

The Montez family had lived on the floor above us, and I knew Allie missed them a lot, even if she never said so.

After they left, I washed the dishes and wiped the counters and the table, all the time hoping the telephone would ring and April would tell me to come over. When the kitchen was cleaned up, I went out on the back porch and waited, still close to the phone.

I was starting to feel a little sleepy when the Danners' door opened and April waved. I hurried across the lawn and went up the steps two at a time. A harsh, grating sound came from inside the house.

"He's using a hacksaw on the lock," April said. "Mr. Kromner wouldn't give him the key. He said he'd have to get permission from the bank that handles the trust, and he hadn't had time to do it. He was still mad about being called in the middle of the night."

"Let's go downstairs," I said. "I want to be there when he opens the door."

April held back. "Maybe you do, but I don't," she said. "There could be something horrible in there." She shuddered.

"But I can't go by myself," I wailed. "You said —"

"I said I'd let you know when he was going to open the door, that's all." She went into the living room and sat on the loveseat. "I just want this to be over," she said and leaned back, her face pale and beautiful against the dark velvet.

"If there's something horrible behind the door, I should think you'd want to be there," I said desperately. "If it was *my* father —"

That was as far as I got. There was a howl of pain from the basement, and the sawing stopped. April leaped up and we both ran to the basement door, just in time to see Mr. Danner stumbling up the stairs. He was clutching one hand in the other, and his white shirtfront was streaked with blood.

THIRTEEN

"Stupid saw!"

Mr. Danner gritted the words and then crumpled to his knees at the top of the stairs. When I helped him up, he was trembling. Together we staggered into the kitchen and I dragged a chair to the sink.

"Hold your hand under the cold-water tap," I said, and he did what he was told, like a little kid. Like Allie, to be exact. If I hadn't cleaned up her scrapes and cuts for years, I suppose I would have been shaking as hard as he was.

The water gushed over the cut. It was a deep one, between his thumb and index finger. He'd need stitches, but first I knew we had to stop the bleeding.

"Where are your towels?" I asked April. That was when I discovered she wasn't even in the kitchen. "Hey, April!"

She appeared at the hall door, as pale as her father.

"Towels!" I said again. "Where are they?"

She edged along the kitchen counter, staying as far away from us as possible. "Middle drawer," she mumbled.

"Call Mike Burton and tell him your dad needs a ride to the emergency room," I told her.

She didn't move. "I don't know the number."

"Look it up!" I exclaimed. Then I had a better idea. "Run over there and tell him — it'll be just as quick."

She moved then, and I could see she was grateful for the chance to get away.

When she was gone, Mr. Danner leaned against the edge of the sink. "Good thing you're here," he said. "I feel pretty queasy. Stupid saw!"

I told him he'd better put his head between his knees, and after that we just waited, not talking. I heard the Burtons' car start, and moments later Mike thumped up the front porch steps and into the house.

When he saw Mr. Danner's bloody shirt and my clumsy-looking bandage, he whistled through his teeth.

"Car's out in front," he said. He helped Mr. Danner to his feet.

At the living room door, Mr. Danner held back and scowled at the bandage. "Mustn't drip," he said. His voice was thick. "Oriental rug — cost a fortune."

"It's okay," Mike said. "Your nurse did a good job." He smiled at me and then cocked his head toward the porch. "You may have another patient out there, Jenny," he said. "I think April could use a glass of water — or something!"

I found an ice-cube tray in the refrigerator and filled a glass with tap water. By the time I got to the front porch, Mike's car had disappeared around the curve of Crescent Lane.

April sat on the top step. "Your dad's okay," I said. "The cut bled a lot, but it wasn't very deep."

"Are you sure?" She sipped the water. "I'd die if that happened to me. It's the worst thing I can think of." She looked down at her hands and shuddered.

Now that was amazing, I thought. No matter where you started with April, she ended up thinking about her violin. If something happened to one of her hands, she really would want to die.

I changed the subject. "Do you think he got the door open before he hurt himself?" I asked.

She shrugged, still staring at her fingers.

"We could go down and find out," I suggested. "You know, just look around a little."

That got her attention. "You're kidding," she snapped.

"I'll go by myself if you don't want to," I said. "But you're the one the crying woman has been bothering. I should think you'd want —"

"Well, I don't!" she said. She looked like a ghost herself, white-faced and miserable.

I stood up and went back into the house alone. Her father was hurt and her mother had walked out, I reminded myself. She was scared. But for both those reasons, I thought she should want to know what was happening in the basement. It was hard to believe she'd rather sulk.

I went through the house to the back hall and waited at the top of the basement stairs, hoping she'd come after me. When she didn't, I started down. There was a flashlight with some other stuff on a little ledge above the steps. I picked up the light. I knew there were a couple of hanging bulbs in the basement, but they wouldn't give nearly enough light in a room full of big, sheet-covered furniture.

"I'm going downstairs now," I yelled. April didn't answer.

I almost turned back, when I reached the bottom. Blood dotted the floor in front of me, and there were a couple of red streaks across the nearest sheet. I edged along one wall; it seemed safer somehow than walking between those hulking shapes.

The basement was so still it hummed. When I reached the far wall, I saw that it was made of rough, painted boards and was mostly hidden by the furniture and boxes piled in front of it. In the center, a space had been cleared around a door made of the same wood. It had oversized black hinges, and there had been a padlock holding it shut. The mangled lock lay on the floor.

I'd been getting more frightened with every step. Now, staring at the broken lock and the blood spattered around, I didn't know if I dared to go any farther. I could go back upstairs and *make* April come with me. Or I could wait for Mr. Danner and Mike to return. I didn't have to do this alone. But then those words — our house, our house — started up in my head again, and I knew I couldn't wait. The crying woman had to be connected with the weird things happening in our house. She was part of whatever was scaring the Carpeks, too. I was sure of it.

There was no doorknob, and at first, when I tugged on the shattered crosspiece of the lock, the door didn't move. I pulled harder and it opened a crack, squeaking loudly. A spider skittered out.

I pulled some more, and when the opening was about ten inches wide, I switched on the flashlight. Holding my breath, I peeked in. All I could see was a triangle of dusty floor; beyond that the darkness was like another wall. The air smelled musty.

I leaned forward without actually stepping inside. The space beyond the wall was narrow, no more than six feet deep. It was like a long closet, I thought. I leaned farther and turned the flashlight one way, then the other, letting the beam move slowly across the floor. At first I didn't see anything except dust — and another spider. Then the light touched the slanting legs of a sawhorse. I moved the light upward, and my heart stopped. I mean, it really did stop! Because there was a second sawhorse beyond the first one, and lying across the two of them was a long box. It looked like a coffin.

I leaped back into the basement. My hands shook so hard I almost dropped the flashlight.

Okay, you've looked, I told myself. That's enough!

Footsteps sounded overhead. "What are you doing, Jenny?" April called. "Are you okay?"

"I've found something," I called back. "Come on down and see."

She ignored that, but she didn't return to the living room, either. Knowing she was there at the top of the stairs made me a tiny bit braver. With the flashlight clutched in both hands, the way policemen hold their guns on crime shows, I stepped through the doorway of the hidden room.

The sawhorses were about four feet to the left of the door. I moved toward them slowly, remembering a "haunted" house Dad took me to one Halloween. There had been a coffin in the living room, and each time a visitor came close to it, the "corpse" sat up and laughed. This coffin looked like that one, though it wasn't quite as long or as deep. The top half was hinged.

Was I scared? *Scared* is just a word. It doesn't tell you I was shivering and sweating at the same time, but I was. I thought I was going to throw up right there in the Danners' basement! *Scared* doesn't tell you that the only dead person I'd ever seen was my mom, and I saw her for just a second before I squeezed my eyes shut, knowing she wouldn't wake up no matter how much I wanted her. I would have been sick then, if Dad hadn't been next to me with his arm tight around my shoulders. This time I was all alone in a dark, spidery place full of secrets. Was I scared? What do you think?

It took awhile before I was able to make myself look inside the box. But I finally did. I held the flashlight in my left hand and hooked the fingers of my right hand under the edge of the lid. It lifted easily.

What I saw first was a lot of pink satin. The box was lined with it, and there was a pink pillow on which something lay. I was so braced for horrors that I thought it was a skull; then I realized it was a circle of flowers, dried brown and held together with wire. Below the pillow, on the bed of satin, lay a white dress trimmed in lace, with a row of tiny buttons down the front. The long sleeves had been folded to meet at the waistline, and a dry-as-dust bouquet of flowers had been placed where they came together, as if invisible hands held them.

I don't know how long I stood looking into the box, stunned by the strangeness of it, but relieved that what lay there was a dress, not a body. Then a sob, no louder than a whisper, made me jump. I let the lid of the box drop and swung the flashlight beam to the end of the narrow room. No one was there, but the crying grew louder. I backed toward the doorway, and by the time I stepped through it, the sobbing was all around me. It even seemed to be inside my head, nearly drowning out April, who was screaming, "Jenny, what's happening!" from the hall upstairs.

FOURTEEN

I didn't slow down at the top of the stairs. The back door was open, and I dashed out of the house into the fresh air. At the foot of the porch steps I finally stopped, so suddenly that April crashed into me.

"What happened?" she panted. "Did you see the crying woman?"

I waited for my heart to stop pounding.

"She's gone now," April said. I listened. The only sound was the peaceful night-talk of insects in the woods.

"Come on, tell me what you saw!" April demanded. "You have to — it's *our* ghost!"

When had she remembered that? I wondered. I stared into the darkness at the end of the yard, wondering if the moonlight man was lurking there. Then I crossed to the tire-swing and sat down.

"Let's go in your house," April said, following me. "It's spooky out here."

"We have a ghost, too, you know," I reminded her.

She groaned. "Okay, okay! Just tell me what you saw in the basement, will you? Why did you run?"

I told her about the coffin-box, the wedding dress, the dried flowers. Then I described how I'd felt when the crying began — as if all that sadness had crowded around me to peer over my shoulder into the box.

April folded her arms across her chest. "Then you didn't actually see anyone?"

I said, "I didn't have to see her. She was there."

She was impressed, I could tell. "My father will have to burn the dress," she said. "That's the best thing to do. Get rid of the dress and I bet that'll finish it — no more ghost in the basement!"

Burn the dress! I stared at her. We finally had a clue to the mystery and she wanted to burn it!

"You can't do that!" I exclaimed, but before I could list the reasons why not, a car turned into the driveway between our houses. Dad and Allie were home.

"My father should be back by now, too," April said. "Maybe the cut was worse than you thought."

"People have to take their turn in the emergency room," I told her. "You can wait with us if you want to. But don't talk about what happened tonight."

She nodded and headed for our back porch. Allie came running to the swing to tell me Jeffy and Joy Marie had moved to Chicago, and Dad went on into the house. His shoulders sagged as if the trip had depressed him.

"Well, what have you girls been up to?" I heard him ask April in a phony cheerful voice. "Have you had a nice evening?"

Last night I had another spooky dream. I was wandering along a path lined with tall rocks. If I made the right turns, I would find my way out; if I made a wrong one, I was going to see something horrible. I woke up sweating and fell asleep again. This time the rocks had turned into pieces of furniture draped in sheets.

Allie was already dressed when I came down to the kitchen. She looked mournfully through the rain-streaked window and asked, "Do you think Justin's at the playground?"

"If he is, he's pretty soggy by now."

She didn't smile, and I understood how she felt. We both needed cheering up.

"Never mind," I said. "We'll do something fun indoors." And we'll do it upstairs, I added to myself. So far, the footsteps in the hall had only sounded when I was downstairs and alone. After last night, I wasn't ready for another ghost.

There was a box of snapshots in the basement, all jumbled together. I know my mother would have sorted them out if she'd lived, probably filling a photo album for each of us. There were a lot more baby pictures of me than of Allie — Dad sort of forgot about the camera after Mom died — but I was sure we could fill the bulletin board I'd had in my bedroom in our last apartment. It was in the basement, too, since I had nothing new to put on it. That's the trouble with moving: Each time you do it, you have to start your life all over again.

After breakfast, I carried the box up to Allie's room, and she dragged the bulletin board, bumping it on every step. We found some shots of the house we were living in when Allie was born, and one of Mom leaving the hospital with Allie in her arms.

I remember how I felt when we got home that day.

Until then, the baby had been a *thing* we talked about and peeked at through the hospital-nursery window. Now she was in our house, lying on our couch, waving her fists in the air. Neighbors kept coming in to look at her. I understood, finally, that she was going to be with us forever and I wasn't the baby anymore.

Allie listened solemnly while I told her how I'd felt. There were more snaps of Mom holding her, with me leaning against the arm of her chair, and a couple of the two of them on a blanket in the backyard. After that there were no more pictures of Mom, and the shots of Allie and me were from birthday parties and Christmas dinners where other people had cameras. Still, we managed to put together a pretty good picture-story of Allie's life.

When the pictures were mounted, we cut flowers and leaves from construction paper and tacked them in a kind of garland around the frame. Then we hung the board at the foot of her bed where she would see it first thing every morning.

While we worked, I listened for the slam of the Danners' screen door. Mr. Danner had seemed calmer when Mike brought him home from the hospital, but he'd been in a hurry to go inside and lie down. I wondered what he'd thought when April told him about the wedding dress. Would he dare to burn it, when the owners of the house had been so concerned about keeping it safe?

The telephone rang as we finished lunch. It was April, her voice as cool and distant as it had been that first day when she brought her violin from the car to show it to us. The dress was gone, she said, just in case I was wondering. Her father was going to leave it at the real-estate office on his way home from work.

"Why?" It was better than burning it, I thought, but not much.

"Because he doesn't want it around, obviously. He's going to tell Mr. Kromner if the dress is so valuable someone else has to take care of it."

I asked if he was going to keep looking for the "noisy pipe," and she said she guessed he would if they heard it again. "But we won't," she said confidently. "The dress is gone, and that's the end of it."

"Will you tell me what Mr. Kromner says?" I asked.

"Yes, but don't say anything about it to my father." Then she added, "I think he's afraid my mother won't come back," and her voice trembled just a little.

I read all afternoon, lying on my bed, while Allie played with her dolls and watched television. When a car drove into the crescent at about five o'clock we both went out on the porch, thinking Dad might have come home early. Instead it was Mike Burton, waving cheerfully as he pulled up in front of our house.

"How's Bob Danner?"

I told him April's father had gone to work, so he must be okay. Then I asked if he'd had a chance to look for information about the theft at the Trans-Union Trucking Company fifty years ago.

"That's why I stopped, Miss Detective," he said. "According to our files, three people were involved, and one of them — get this — was named David Tate!"

"The man who owned our house?"

"Not likely," Mike said. "His son, probably. All the robbers were eighteen or nineteen. Tate was believed to be the ringleader, but the case never went to trial. David Tate died in a smashup right here on Crescent Lane. The police said he was speeding. After his death, the other boys took investigators to the place where the stolen money was hidden, and soon after that Trans-Union dropped the charges. That's why you didn't see more about it in the *Herald*."

"What's the matter, Jenny?" Allie asked suddenly. "You look funny."

"I'm interested," I told her. "It's very interesting to find out about things that happened a long time ago."

"One more thing." Mike grinned, because he knew

I was trying to hide my excitement. "The last note in our files says Lt. James Carpek received special commendation for his work on the case. I don't imagine the Tates were particularly fond of their policeman neighbor after that. Though they could hardly blame him for doing his job."

I was dizzy trying to sort out all he'd told me. The most important fact, I decided, was that there had been a young man living in our house fifty years ago — a young man who died in a car crash. I couldn't be sure, of course, but it seemed to me that now the moonlight man had a name.

"Does that help, Sherlock?" Mike asked. "Because it's the best I can do."

I wanted to hug him. "It helps a lot!" I said. I thought it might even explain the crying woman in the Danners' basement. Perhaps she had been David Tate's girlfriend. Maybe she'd killed herself when he died! I knew I was letting my imagination run wild!

Mike started to drive away, then stopped and backed up. "I might as well pass on an invitation right now. Kathy and I want to have a neighborhood cookout on the Fourth of July, and we're hoping everyone will be there — including the Carpeks."

"The Fourth of July?" So much had happened in June that I hadn't noticed the month was nearly gone.

"Will there be fireworks?" Allie asked shyly.

"The best!" Mike told her. "The Newton Park Board is going to use your school playground as a launching pad for their fireworks display since it's the highest point on this side of town. We can stay in our own backyard and have the best seats possible!"

Allie's face glowed, and I wanted to hug Mike again. A neighborhood cookout is just what the crescent needs. It's what *we* need — my family and I. People have neighborhood parties when they like where they are.

FIFTEEN

Mr. Danner came home about a half hour later than usual last night, and he was in the house for only ten minutes. When he left, April went with him. I didn't see her again until this evening — didn't hear the violin, either. She told me tonight that they'd gone to her aunt's house to try to talk her mother into coming home.

"She said no." April sounded the way Allie does when she's really, really worried and trying not to show it.

"Did he tell her about the dress?" I asked.

She nodded. "He said the whole ghost business was ridiculous and not worth breaking up over. My mother said if he didn't believe in ghosts why was he so anxious to get rid of the dress? And then she ran upstairs and didn't come down again."

I didn't know what to say.

"It'll be okay," April went on quickly. "They argue, but they get over it." I think she was trying to make both of us believe that.

"What about the dress?" I knew I shouldn't keep asking questions when she was so upset, but I couldn't help it. "What did Mr. Kromner say?"

"He said he didn't know anything about it. A woman named Cora Blake owns our house and some other property, but she's in a nursing home and the bank takes care of her estate. He said no one else has ever complained about noises in the basement, and he said we have to pay for the broken lock. My father says we'd move out tomorrow if we could afford it."

Cora. It was a pretty, old-fashioned name. Romantic. Cora would be the kind of girl who'd lock her wedding dress away in a secret room to hide her broken heart.

"Mike says there was a boy named David Tate living in our house fifty years ago," I said. "He was killed in a car accident on Crescent Lane. Maybe he and Cora were lovers, and when he died she couldn't bear it."

April sniffed. "She did bear it, Jenny," she said. "She's an old lady in a nursing home now — not a ghost."

Just then, Mr. Carpek shuffled around the corner into our backyard. His face was grim, and he was dragging Allie behind him.

"Where's your old man?" he roared, as soon as he saw us. "This happens one more time and I call the cops!"

Allie broke away and threw herself against me so hard that I almost fell. "I didn't do it!" she yelled. "I didn't!"

"Didn't do what?"

"Anything!"

"My father's not home," I told Mr. Carpek, who looked as if he might explode at any second. "He had to go to a meeting. What's wrong?"

"This kid's been banging on our windows, scaring my wife — and it's not the first time, either! Now I catch her ringing our doorbell like crazy. She deserves a good smack!"

"Didn't!" Allie wailed again.

"My sister wouldn't do that," I said, more bravely than I felt. If Mr. Carpek actually smacked Allie, I didn't know what I'd do.

"She was on our steps," he growled. "Why was she there if she didn't ring the bell?"

I unwrapped Allie's arms from around me. "Why?" I asked.

She didn't answer at first. Then she said, "I thought I saw *him* on the porch. The moonlight man. He was looking in a window."

"Who was looking in the window?" Now Mr. Carpek sounded as if he were the one who'd been given a good smack.

"The dog was there, too," Allie said.

"Dog?" Mr. Carpek repeated. "What're you talking about?" The color drained out of his face at the mention of the dog. Then Mrs. Carpek began screaming from inside their house, and he ran toward his door. It was the fastest I'd ever seen him move.

"Go with April," I told Allie, but April had disappeared. "Wait inside," I said, and gave her a little push. "I'll be there in a minute."

"Where're you going?" she asked fearfully.

"To see if Mrs. Carpek is okay." I ran then, even though I knew what happened inside the Carpeks' house was none of my business. If I didn't find out what was wrong, I'd stay awake wondering the rest of the night.

When I stepped through the front door, both Carpeks were in the middle of the living room staring at the television set. A game show was on, and the audience was shouting advice.

"How could that be?" Mrs. Carpek was hanging onto Mr. Carpek's arm. "How could it be there?"

Mr. Carpek snatched up the remote and turned off the set. "It was just a show," he mumbled. "You dreamed it."

"I was locking the windows the way you told me to," she said. She kept staring at the darkened screen. "Then I heard a funny sound in here, as if someone maybe switched the channel. So I came in to see, and it was right there on the screen." She turned to her husband as if she were begging him to believe her but knew he wouldn't. "It was just the way it was that night," she gasped. "Things lying all over — blood —"

That was when Mr. Carpek noticed me.

"You get out," he said. He didn't sound mad anymore, just old and tired. "Who asked you to come in here?"

"I — I thought maybe I could help," I stammered. And he said, "Well, you can't."

It was a relief to get outside again. There was so much unhappiness in that room, I'd felt as if I were suffocating.

SIXTEEN

Facts I've learned in the last two days:

Number One: Allison Joslin is one great kid. (Well, I knew *that* before.) Sure, she's shy — Dad worries about that, but he shouldn't. Behind that shyness she knows what she knows.

"I really did see the moonlight man on the porch," she told me when I was putting her to bed that night. "Just for a minute. And I really did see the dog."

"I believe you," I said. "Mr. Carpek believes you, too. He doesn't want to believe, but he does. I think he's frightened."

"Even if he's old?" She sounded amazed.

"Old people can be as frightened as young ones," I said.

She thought about that, and then she cuddled Sammy close to her and shut her eyes. "We ought to have a real dog," she said softly and fell asleep.

Number Two: The Carpeks *should* be afraid! What's happened to them is a lot worse than footsteps in the hall, whistling, and a disappearing picture. Something dark and cruel made us think we saw Mr. Carpek lying dead in his backyard. The same angry spirit tipped that ladder just as Mr. Carpek was going to step on it. And it made a terrifying picture appear on the Carpeks' television screen. If the moonlight man is David Tate, he may be puzzled to find strangers living in his house, but I don't think we're important to him. He only cares about those two old people next door. They're the reason he's come back.

I went to bed thinking about the eerie scene in the Carpeks' living room, and it was there in my head the next morning, as if I hadn't slept at all. What was the "something horrible" Mrs. Carpek saw on their television? When I tried to guess, my stomach churned the way it does when I have to go to the doctor or give a speech at school.

I went downstairs and found Dad finishing his coffee and Allison fishing for raisins in her cereal. I wondered if she'd told him about Mr. Carpek's temper tantrum and decided she hadn't. If he knew, he'd be knocking on the Carpeks' door right now. And he'd be thinking about moving again. Allie knows him as well as I do!

Our car was the first one to go down the hill, and Mike and Kathy left next. Then Mr. Danner backed out of his driveway so fast his tires spun. After that, the crescent was terribly quiet. Like every other day, I told myself, but for some reason this didn't feel like every other day. The silence hummed, the way it had in the Danners' basement just before I found the wedding dress.

Our neighbors on both sides had their windows closed tight, even though the day was warm. April was practicing by this time and didn't want to be accused of disturbing the peace again. I wondered if the Carpeks were okay.

"Is Mr. Carpek outside?" Allie asked nervously.

I told her there was no sign of him. "Do you want to play in the yard?"

"I'd rather go to the playground," she said. "You come, too." She was going to need a couple of days at least to forgive Mr. Carpek.

We spent the whole morning there. Allie raced around with Justin and her other friends, and I sat near the edge of the woods, reading and soaking up sun. This is the first summer I've gotten a real tan. My skin is getting dark and my hair is getting lighter. Dad says I look more like Mom now, which I like to hear, even though he sounds sort of lost when he says it. I think looking like her is a sign that she would have approved of our new house and wanted us to stay there. She would have wanted me to fight for it!

But what could I do? At twelve-thirty I called Allie and we went home for lunch. I thought hard while we ate our sandwiches — peanut butter and banana for Allie, cheese and pickle for me — but I kept coming up against dead ends. The Carpeks weren't going to tell me what happened fifty years ago. Mike Burton had reported all he could find in the newspaper files. And the wedding dress was gone. I wished I'd been brave enough to examine it when I'd had the chance. There might have been a note tucked into the sleeve or a name sewn into a hem.

A name . . . Suddenly, I realized I *did* have a name! Mr. Kromner had told April's father that their house belonged to Cora Blake. She would know about the dress. All I had to do was find her!

The telephone directory listed three nursing homes in Newton. The first one I called had a patient named John Blake. No Cora. The woman who answered at the second one sounded as if she had more important things to do than answer questions about patients. I gave her Cora Blake's name and waited. I think she must have poured herself a cup of coffee, and maybe she drank it, too. Just when I was going to hang up and try the third number she came back and said yes, they did have a Cora Blake, but she didn't have a telephone in her room, and was there anything *else* I wanted. The telephone clicked off as soon as I said no.

I told Allie we were going to town, which pleased her and made her suspicious at the same time. She definitely didn't want to go to that real-estate office again. And she didn't feel like waiting around in the library while I read old newspapers.

"This time we're going to visit a lady who used to live in April's house," I told her. "She'll tell us what it was like here when she was young."

"Or we could go back to the playground," Allie suggested. But she didn't argue when I said I'd had enough sun. Ten minutes later we were on our way.

It was the second time we'd walked down Crescent Lane since the day the dog had come out of the woods. "What if he comes again?" Allie asked, without saying who *he* was.

"We'll just keep on going," I said. "We have as much right to be on this road as any silly old dog."

That sounded a lot bolder than I felt, but I couldn't let the moonlight man and his pet stop us. We walked down the hill, going a little faster as we rounded each curve and saw nothing but empty road ahead of us. By the time we reached the bottom we were running, and laughing, too.

Maybe I'd been wrong this morning, I thought; maybe this was going to be just another nice summer day.

The bus took us right to the door of the Southridge Care Center. I wasn't looking forward to meeting the woman who'd answered my call an hour earlier. She was probably the kind of grown-up who enjoyed telling kids they weren't allowed in without their parents. But when we crossed the lobby, which was sunny and so shiny-clean it made my eyes ache, there was a man at the front desk talking on the phone. He kept the receiver to his ear, smiling and shaking his head, while he looked up Cora Blake's room number and pointed down a cluttered hall.

Allie took one look and tried to pull me back across the lobby. "Let's see the lady some other time," she said. "Maybe tomorrow."

"Today," I said firmly. "It won't take long."

We walked along the hall checking the numbers painted on each door. Some of the bedrooms were bright and cheerful, with pictures on the walls and quilted bedspreads. In others the curtains were drawn, and the patients who lay in the beds all looked alike — thin and waxy-faced. A few people sat in wheelchairs in the hall, and some of them smiled at Allie and said hello. She smiled back, until one old lady, clutching a stuffed cat, reached out and tried to touch her.

"Let's go *home*," she whispered then.

"If we had a grandma, she'd be about as old as that lady," I said. "And about as lonesome, if she was living in this place." I knew it wasn't fair to make her feel guilty when she was frightened, but by then we were just a few doors from Room 127. I couldn't bear to leave without talking to Cora Blake.

The way things turned out, we didn't talk to her, anyway. Room 127 was one of the darkened ones — shades pulled, no television set. The old lady lying in the bed had hair like dandelion fluff, and there was an oxygen mask covering part of her face. The hands that lay on the sheet were the thinnest I'd ever seen.

"Is she dead?" Allie whispered fearfully.

"She's sleeping," I said. "But she must be pretty

sick, or she wouldn't be getting oxygen. I don't know if we should wake her —"

"Couldn't if you tried," a voice said behind us. A big woman wearing blue pants and a white jacket pushed past us and went to the bed. She adjusted the oxygen mask and checked an intravenous bag hanging from a pole. "You can come in if you want to," she said over her shoulder. "But it's no use trying to talk to Cora. She's been like this for weeks, poor thing. Are you relatives?"

I shook my head. "We're neighbors — sort of. Her house is next to ours." We watched her lift Cora Blake's head to fluff her pillow. "Do you think we could come back another day — maybe next week?"

"Come back as often as you want," the woman said. "Won't make a bit of difference — nobody expects her to wake up. She's peaceful enough most of the time, but not always. You can tell she's havin' bad dreams sometimes inside her poor head. I've come in and seen tears runnin' down her cheeks." She looked at us thoughtfully and added, "Better not to bother her, if you ask me." She scooped up a pile of towels from a chair and brushed past us again, giving Allie a tap on the head as she left.

"Okay, we're leaving," I said quickly, before Allie

could start again. "The nurse is right, we shouldn't bother her." It was another dead end.

We walked down the hall, dodging carts loaded with trays, trying not to get in anyone's way. I was surprised when Allie's hand suddenly slipped out of mine.

I turned around and saw that she'd stopped in front of the lady who had tried to touch her earlier. "Come on, Allison," I said. "Let's go."

She didn't move. "I like your kitty," she said finally. "He's pretty. I have a bear named Sammy."

The old lady's expression didn't change, and I knew she hadn't forgiven Allie for pulling away from her earlier. But then she smiled just a little.

"Sammy is a nice name for a bear," she said. And she held out her cat so Allie could pet it.

SEVENTEEN

We were halfway home when the rain started — another reason to wish we hadn't come to town. I'd been uptight when I woke this morning, but that was nothing compared to the way I felt after visiting Cora Blake. I'd wanted her to be a sweet old lady who would tell us her secrets as soon as she understood why we needed them. It had never occurred to me that Cora might be too sick to talk.

By the time we stepped down from the bus at Crescent Lane, a river of rain was racing along the curb.

"We're going to get all wet, Jenny," Allie complained. "We should've gone to Daddy's store to wait for him." I agreed. The trouble was, when we left the nursing home I hadn't noticed the black, puffy clouds piling up in the west. I'd just wanted to get away.

"A little bit of rain won't hurt," I told her. "Just because Dad calls you Sugar doesn't mean you'll melt."

I started up the road, but she didn't move. "I'd rather wait," she insisted. "Daddy will come soon."

I glanced at my watch. "Not for a half hour, at least. If we walk fast, we'll be home in five minutes."

She gave up then but stayed a couple of steps behind me to show she didn't approve. "It's raining harder," she pointed out, after we'd walked for a few minutes.

I pretended not to hear. I made myself remember how I'd felt, riding high in the cab of the U-Haul, the first time we drove up this road. Of course, the view was a lot different in the rain. It didn't matter. This was still our woods. It was still our road leading to our house.

Allie heard the car first. "Daddy's coming," she said happily.

I listened. A car had started up Crescent Lane, moving fast. Tires screamed on the curves.

"That's not Dad!" I exclaimed. I grabbed Allie's hand and jumped into the tall grass at the side of the road, just as the car came shrieking into sight. It barely made the turn, then skidded toward us. Allie screamed, and we both leaped backward into a ditch that was partly filled with water. Above us, a horn blared and there was more squealing of tires. I held my breath, waiting for a crash that didn't come. Instead, the motor's roar faded as suddenly as it had begun. The road was still again, except for the patter of raindrops.

We climbed out of the ditch. "That was the same car," Allie said. Her teeth chattered. "It was the car in the picture, Jenny."

I stared at her, wishing she didn't sound so certain. I'd had only a quick glimpse before we went into the ditch, but it had been enough to see that the car was a convertible. The top had been down, and I thought there was only one person in it, though I couldn't be sure.

"The boy in the picture was driving," Allie said. She hiccuped, holding back tears.

"You can't know that," I told her.

She ignored me. "How are we going to get home?" she demanded. "What if he's waiting around the curve?"

I didn't know what to do. The car had to be up there ahead of us. We were nearly to the top of the hill, but the last curve was a sharp one. It was terrifying to think the convertible might be waiting, just out of sight.

I stood there trying to think, with Allie clutching my wet T-shirt. Then I heard another car start up the hill. This one was noisy, too, but it was a familiar noisiness.

"It's okay, that's Mike," I told Allie. But I held my breath until the green sedan came around the curve.

Mike stopped and leaned out the window. "What are you doing here, for Pete's sake? Come on, get in."

"We can't," I said. "We'll ruin the upholstery."

He laughed. "Too late for that," he said. "It was ruined before we bought it."

We climbed into the backseat, and he drove slowly around the curve. The road was empty. When we reached the crescent, there was still no car in sight. Allie sighed, and I knew what she was thinking. Not finding the car at the top of the hill was almost worse than seeing it there. Where could it have gone?

"Okay, you two," Mike said, as he stopped in front of our house. "You didn't get that muddy walking in the rain. What happened?"

I took a deep breath. "We had to jump to get out of the way of a car," I told him. "It was speeding and it skidded and —"

He looked around the crescent. "What car was

that? Couldn't have been Carpek — he never speeds. And Danner —"

"It wasn't them," Allie interrupted. "It was the car in the picture in my room. A car without a top."

"Top down in this weather?" Mike frowned at her, then at me. "What's going on here?"

At that moment April came out on her porch. I didn't want to ask her for a favor after the way she'd sneaked off when Mr. Carpek was yelling at Allie, but I had to talk to Mike alone.

"Ask April if they have any cocoa," I said, giving Allie a little push. "That's what we need to warm up."

"We have cocoa," Allie said. But when I reached around her to open the car door, she slid out. As soon as she was gone, I told Mike what had happened.

"I know it sounds impossible," I said. "But we really did see the car, and we heard it, too. Allie says it's the car in the picture that keeps appearing and disappearing on her bedroom wall."

This is it, I thought when I'd finished. This is where he tells me to grow up. This is where he says he was wrong about my being a good reporter. I waited, watching raindrops splat against the windshield and race to the bottom of the glass.

"I told you and Kathy all the weird stuff that's been happening," I said finally. "Lots of it —"

He held up his hand. "Let's deal with one piece of weird stuff at a time," he said. "Do you think this mysterious car and David Tate are connected in some way? The reason I'm asking is because I'm trying to remember something. When we talked about Tate, did I mention the date of his death? Did I?"

"I — I don't think so." I shivered.

"I don't think I did, either," he said. He cocked his head at me with a funny little smile. "But I'm almost sure it was July second — fifty years ago today. If a person wanted to believe in ghosts, that would be interesting. This is an anniversary."

Interesting? That was a pretty wimpy word for it. This was the anniversary of the moonlight man's death! No wonder this day had felt different.

Allie came out the Danners' front door with a plastic container in her hand. As I started to get out of the car, Mike reached across to pat my shoulder.

"We'll go over all that other weird stuff again soon," he said. "I'm beginning to think it would make a great story for the *Herald*. But in the meantime, don't worry too much about what you think you saw, Jenny. You might have imagined the whole thing. The woods can be spooky in the rain, right?"

I slid out of the car and ran up the steps to unlock

the front door. At least he hadn't laughed. He even believed me, sort of. But I'll tell you this, if he expects to write a newspaper story about the haunted crescent, he isn't going to get any help from me. I don't want him turning our house into a freaky sideshow for people to stare at!

EIGHTEEN

Shut out your thoughts the way you shut a door. You'll be asleep in no time.

Dad says that usually works for him, but I've never gotten the hang of it. One little thought after another sneaks in before I can stop them. Last night was the worst. I kept seeing that car skid toward us on the wet road. Then I thought about Cora Blake lying in her dark room, and I imagined tears rolling down her cheeks. And I kept hearing Mike say, "This is an anniversary."

A couple of times, I got up and tiptoed down the hall to Allie's bedroom to look out her window. The rain had turned to drizzle, and our backyard was completely dark. David Tate was out there — I was sure of it, even if I couldn't see him. He might be looking up at me. He might be getting ready to throw pebbles at Cora's window or tap on the Carpeks' door. Or he could be planning something much worse, since this was an anniversary.

The second time I got up, Dad came out of his bedroom. I jumped, and so did he.

"Why are you prowling around?" he whispered. Before I could think of an answer, he said, "I'm going downstairs to watch TV for a while. I can't sleep, either."

"Shut your mind the way you shut a door," I teased, but he just snorted. I followed him to the kitchen, where he picked up a glass of milk and a piece of cake. Then we went into the living room.

"Something's wrong with Allison," he said grumpily. "She's too quiet."

"She's always quiet," I said.

He picked up the television remote and put it down again. "She acts worried," he said. "Why should she be worried? Do you think she's unhappy here?"

I braced myself. "She loves it here," I said. "So do I. It's just that . . ."

"Just what?"

"Nothing," I said. How could I even think of telling *him* the truth?

"I bet Allie's lonely," he said. "I should have given that more thought before we moved way up here. It's different for you — you've been lucky to find a friend next door."

Some friend! I thought. This was not the time to tell him April and I were hardly speaking.

"Allie has friends," I said. "We go to the playground almost every day. She has a boyfriend, remember?"

I hoped he'd smile at that, but he didn't. That despairing look was one I'd seen many times before. And we hadn't even lived in the crescent for a full month!

"We both love it here," I repeated, to drown out the terrible thing he might be going to say next. It was a relief when he shook his head and switched on the television set. He wasn't ready to talk about moving right now, but I knew, as sure as we were sitting there, he was beginning to think about it.

I went back to bed, and this time I didn't even try to sleep. Allie had been badly scared this afternoon — as scared as I was! — but she hadn't mentioned the car after we changed our clothes and drank some cocoa. I think she was counting on me — and maybe

Mike Burton — to make everything all right. So what was it, I wondered, that had convinced Dad she was unhappy? Could he feel danger in the crescent, even though he'd never seen the moonlight man? Or was his restlessness the same old thing — loneliness for Mom?

April came over after breakfast this morning — that was a surprise! I was making chocolate-chip cookies from a mix when she tapped on the screen. I invited her to sit down and wait for the first batch to bake.

"Guess what," she said, while I checked to see if we had any more lemonade.

"The crying woman is back?"

"No way."

"Your mother's coming home?"

"Tomorrow," she said. "My father convinced her she's being silly. And I think my aunt needs the spare bedroom for someone else."

I poured the lemonade and waited to hear more.

"Mr. Cargio made a tape and sent it to Jacob Mindler. He's the teacher in Chicago I told you about," she added impatiently. "And he's going to take me as his pupil — I don't even have to compete. It's all settled!"

She was so pleased that it was impossible not to be

happy with her. The cool, sulky expression was gone; she looked as if a light had been turned on inside of her.

"That's great!" I said. "Congratulations!"

"Starting in September I'll take the train to Chicago every Saturday morning," she said. "Studying with Jacob Mindler is the best thing that could possibly happen to me."

She didn't say nothing else mattered, but I knew it was true. Jacob Mindler made up for the way her parents fought all the time, and for having to move from their beautiful big house to a crowded little one. Her family, the Carpeks, the moonlight man, the neighbors — we were *all* shadows. Mr. Mindler was real.

"That's great!" I said again. "You're going to be famous."

April smiled. "Not for a while," she said modestly. "I have a lot of hard work ahead of me."

She stayed till the cookies were baked. She even said they were good, though I'm sure she wouldn't have noticed if they were burned black. When she left, she sort of floated out of the kitchen, and I sat there by myself feeling totally blah. Chocolate-chip cookies! I thought. Some talent! They weren't even made from scratch.

Then Allie came running downstairs with a picture she'd drawn. It was our house — a little lopsided maybe, but with a rainbow of flowers around the front porch.

"Let's plant a garden," she said. "The kind of flowers that keep coming up every year."

"Perennials," I said. And I hugged her, reassured that I'd told Dad the truth. Allie did love our house and wanted to stay here.

I made sandwiches to go with the cookies, and after lunch we went through the woods to the playground. A couple of pickup trucks stood on the lawn, and a half-dozen workmen were hammering and sawing.

"What are they building?" Allie asked.

I wondered, too. Then I remembered what Mike had said when he invited us to the cookout.

"I bet it's a platform for people to stand on while they set off the Fourth of July fireworks," I said. "That way, no one else can get too close."

We watched for a while, or rather, I did; Allie watched for Justin. When the sky clouded over, we went home again and wandered around the crescent's backyards, trying to figure out exactly where we would stand to get the best view of the rockets as they exploded above the trees.

"Maybe next year the cookout will be at our house," I suggested. "It'll become a neighborhood tradition."

"And everyone will say our garden is pretty," Allie said. "Do you think we can have a pond with goldfish?"

We stared at each other, and I wondered whether she'd possibly overheard Dad talk about her last night. I didn't know how she could have, but still she knew. I guess she'd recognized the look on his face, the same as I did.

I pointed at an evergreen tree at the end of the yard, near the woods. "Next Christmas we'll put lights on that one," I said firmly. "And we'll put out food for the birds."

A door opened behind us, and when we turned around Mrs. Carpek was on her back porch. She had a rug in her hands, as if she'd come outside to shake it, but instead she just stared into space.

"Let's run," Allie whispered. She wanted nothing to do with the Carpeks, and I didn't blame her. But there was something really sad about the way the old lady stood there, her shoulders slumped, the rug dragging on the porch as if she'd forgotten about it.

I called "Hi," wondering if she'd pretend not to

hear, but instead she lifted a hand in a little wave. "I made cookies," she called hoarsely. "You want some?"

"Tell her we have our own cookies," Allie muttered, but I shushed her fast. This was Mrs. Carpek talking! Actually being friendly!

"Go in the house, Allie," I said. "It's going to rain any minute. Draw more pictures. How about a picture of our Fourth of July cookout and the birds' Christmas tree? You can show them to Dad tonight."

She took off, pleased with that assignment, and I walked across the lawn. As I got close to Mrs. Carpek, I saw that her eyes were puffy and red behind her glasses.

I must have looked nervous, because she said, "He isn't here," as I climbed the porch steps. "He always has errands in town. Or he has to take a walk. Anything to get out of the house!"

She draped the rug over the railing and led the way inside, closing the door behind us. The wind had been picking up, but Mrs. Carpek's windows were closed. It was so warm in the kitchen that I could hardly breathe.

"Peanut-butter cookies," Mrs. Carpek said, pointing to a jar on the counter. "Help yourself."

The cookie jar was in the shape of a little house. I

lifted the roof and took out a couple of cookies, trying not to notice that tears were running down Mrs. Carpek's cheeks. She didn't seem to notice them, either.

"He leaves me here alone and says, 'Don't you talk to anybody,' so I don't," she said bitterly. "It's better that way, he says, and I thought so, too. But this summer is different. Bad things happen every day! He knows, and he leaves me alone, anyway."

I sat still as a stone, with a zillion questions I didn't dare ask.

"Why am I talking?" she exclaimed suddenly. "You're just a kid. You can't do anything."

"I can listen," I said cautiously. "And I sort of know how you feel, Mrs. Carpek. Strange things have happened at our house, too. And at the Danners'. I wish I understood what was going on."

She eyed me suspiciously. "What kind of strange things?"

"Whistling. Footsteps. A man walking around our backyard, only he isn't a real man —"

"That's Tate," she said at once, and I felt my heart stop. "I told Arthur he's back, but he says I'm crazy. I even saw him on the television — that night you were here with that other girl. The fiddle player."

"You saw David Tate on television?" I forgot I wasn't supposed to know who she was talking about, but she didn't notice.

"I saw his accident, that's what. The car all crumpled up, and him lying on the road. It was there for just a second, whether Arthur believes me or not!" She was crying again, but she sounded angry, too.

"Well, I believe you," I said. "I think David Tate is trying to scare all of us — especially you and Mr. Carpek. I just don't understand why."

She took a large man's handkerchief from her apron pocket and twisted it into a ball. "He thinks it was our fault," she said in a raspy whisper, as if she could hardly bear to say the words out loud. "They all did!"

"The accident was your fault?"

"Everything!" she said. "Everything that happened that summer. They blamed us, and it's not fair. He brought it on himself!"

NINETEEN

"**H**e brought what on himself, Mrs. Carpek?" I asked. "What do you mean?" I thought I'd die right there in that hot little kitchen if she didn't keep talking.

Her eyes flicked toward the back door, as if she expected her husband to pop in at any moment.

"Well, I'll tell you this," she said in a hoarse whisper. "That boy — that David — was bad. A real no-gooder! He talked smart and he drove too fast and he couldn't hold a job. He claimed the bosses had it in for him, but we knew better. Arthur said he was a no-gooder the day the Tates moved in. He fooled his folks for sure, and he fooled the Blakes, too. They thought the whole town was picking on him. But he never fooled us!"

"The Blakes?" I repeated, as if I were having trouble keeping the story straight.

"They built the house that fiddle player lives in," Mrs. Carpek said. "The Blakes and the Tates moved here about the same time. They were buddy-buddy right away, the parents and the kids. Cora Blake — I don't think she ever had a boyfriend before. She was a nice girl — way too nice for David Tate! From the first day, they were together all the time. It was a shame, and I told Arthur so. Someone ought to put an end to that, I said."

Mrs. Carpek had stopped worrying about saying too much. Her little eyes glittered like black beads, and she breathed hard, as if the thought of David and Cora together still disgusted her after fifty years.

"What happened to them?" I asked.

"What happened was a *robbery*!" She spat out the word. "The trucking company where Edgar Tate — David's father — worked was broken into, and someone saw David's flashy car a block away when it happened. Arthur was a police officer, and he was assigned to question the boy. Arthur could tell right away that he was involved. David admitted it, finally — said he'd planned the whole thing because he needed money to get married. And then, after he'd confessed, he said he wanted to give the money back. Can you believe that? He said he'd made a dumb mistake and he was sorry. He was sorry! The only thing he was sorry about was being caught! He thought since we were neighbors and all, Arthur would help him."

The soft, gurgling sound might have started then — I'm not sure. It was very faint, and I wasn't thinking about anything except what Mrs. Carpek was telling me.

"He almost got away with it, too!" she went on. "Arthur arrested him, and he was in jail overnight. Then the big shots at the trucking company heard who had been arrested, and they sent their lawyers to hush up the whole thing. Maybe Edgar Tate got down on his knees to them — I don't know. Whatever, they dropped the charges. That was a mistake, but it's what they wanted."

She jumped up and paced around the kitchen. "Arthur came home in a state that night, I can tell you!" she exclaimed. "He went through the house swearing and carrying on something awful. I finally told him, if the trucking people won't see that the boy gets what he deserves, the least you can do is warn that poor girl and her parents about what she's getting into. It was the decent thing to do."

I closed my eyes. As clearly as if I'd been there, I could see Mr. Carpek marching across our backyards to the Blakes' house, determined to make David Tate look as bad as possible. I could see Mrs. Carpek watching from the porch and cheering him on.

"So they called off the wedding?" I suggested.

"Of course they did!" she snapped. "Cora never saw the boy again. By the time his father brought him home from jail the next day, Mrs. Blake and Cora were on their way to California to stay with relatives, and Gerald Blake was waiting for him on their front porch. We heard them all yelling at each other — you couldn't *not* hear! Then David ran to that car of his and went screeching down the hill like a banshee. His folks tried to stop him, but he didn't pay them any mind. We were all out there in front when it happened — the crash. We ran down the hill and there he was — in the middle of the road." Her voice quavered, but only for a second. "It was his own fault! Anyone could see that. They had no right to turn on us."

"Who?" I asked. "Who turned on you?"

"All of them," Mrs. Carpek said bitterly. "Edgar Tate quit his job the next week and they moved out of town — who knows where! I don't blame them for wanting to leave, but they had nothing but black looks for Arthur and me before they left. The Blakes stayed on, and Cora lived there alone after her folks died, and all those years the three of them acted as if they didn't know we were here. Just because Arthur told them what they didn't want to know! David Tate was wicked —"

She hesitated. The sound we'd been ignoring was suddenly very loud — a rushing, bubbling waterfall overhead.

"No!" Mrs. Carpek gasped. "No, no, no!"

I ran to the front hall and looked up. Water was splashing over the uncarpeted stairs.

"Make it stop!" Mrs. Carpek shrieked. "Make it stop this minute!"

I thought she meant me, but as I raced up the stairs, I realized I wasn't the one she was screaming at. "You have no right!" she yelled. "It was all your own fault!"

By the time I reached the bathroom, my sneakers were soaked. Both the cold- and hot-water taps were turned on, in the sink and in the bathtub. The faucets were jammed; I needed both hands to shut them. I turned off the sink taps first; they turned themselves back on while I was struggling with the bathtub. I wondered how much of the water had seeped into the floor and would find its way through the downstairs ceilings.

Mrs. Carpek was still screaming when the front doorbell began to ring. The bell was much louder than ours, or maybe it seemed louder because I was so scared. I turned off the sink faucets again and ran back to the top of the stairs.

TWENTY

I've heard that a nightmare lasts only a few seconds — even if it seems to go on forever. What happened at the Carpeks' this afternoon was like that — but different in one big way. When a nightmare gets too scary, sometimes you can wake yourself up.

I looked down at Mrs. Carpek. She was peering through the oval glass in the front door and shaking her fists.

"Go away!" she cried. "Leave us alone!"

I ran down, slipping a couple of times on the wet stairs. There was no one on the porch, but the bell kept ringing. When I reached for the doorknob, Mrs. Carpek grabbed my hand. "Don't you let him in!" she shrieked. "Don't let him in!"

As if we could keep him out! Behind us, water still gushed down the stairs — the entrance hall was a puddle! And there was a scary scorched smell in the air. I raced back to the kitchen. All four burners on the stove top were turned on high, and a couple of hotpads, lying on the stove between the burners, had caught fire. They burned like tiny bonfires, tossing sparks into the air.

I switched off the gas jets and rushed to the sink just as lightning lit up the windows. A dishcloth floated in an overflowing pan; I grabbed it and dropped it over the hotpads. By then the jets were burning again. Mrs. Carpek watched me, her sobs almost drowned out by the doorbell.

I turned off the jets a second time. "Stay here," I shouted at Mrs. Carpek and started toward the front door.

She pulled me back. "You can't leave me," she wailed. "Don't leave me with him!"

"I won't," I shouted. "But we can't even call for help with that noise —" I gestured toward the door and she let me go.

The first drops of rain began to fall as I looked

again through the oval glass. Lightning flared across the crescent, and there must have been thunder, too, but the doorbell was louder. I felt trapped — by the storm and the awful noise and by not knowing what might happen if I opened the door and covered the bell with my hand. Would I feel the moonlight man's fingers, invisible but cold, under mine? I was trying to get up my courage when a pair of headlights appeared around the curve.

For one horrible moment I was sure David Tate's car had come back. Then I recognized the mail carrier's small white truck. It stopped in front of the Burtons' house, and the mailman jumped out and ran up on their porch with a package. Seeing him made me brave. I opened the door.

The ringing stopped. Now there was no sound at all except the drum of rain on the porch roof. I think that sudden silence was the scariest moment of all. I whirled around and looked up the stairs, knowing before I saw him that the moonlight man would be there.

The upstairs hall was dark, but he was darker, his legs apart, his head bent. I couldn't see his face, but I knew he was glaring at me. Rage poured down the stairs, as real as the waterfall had been.

"Is everything okay in there?"

It was the mailman. He'd moved his truck up to the Carpeks' mailbox and was peering anxiously at me through the rain.

I looked up the stairs again. The hall was empty. Then Mrs. Carpek crowded in front of me.

"It's all right," she called to the mailman. "We got plumbing troubles. My husband will fix it." She waved him on and then turned to me. "You go, too," she said breathlessly. "Before Arthur comes home. It's over — I can tell."

When I didn't move, she gave me a push. "Go," she said. "And don't make a big story of this business — I know how you kids are. It wasn't true, that stuff I told you. I made it up." She looked at the water-soaked stairway with a sick expression. "Go!" she said again. "Don't talk."

I went. The rain was coming down harder than ever, but it was such a relief to get away from the heat and craziness in that little house that I stood out in the road and let the rain wash over me for a couple of minutes. I might have stayed longer, but another set of headlights swung into the crescent. Mr. Carpek turned into his driveway without looking at me.

I wondered what he'd say when his wife told him

what had just happened. Probably the same kind of thing she'd said to me: *It isn't true. Don't make a big story out of nothing.*

I went home and found April in our kitchen drinking lemonade with Allie.

"Our lights went out," April explained. "I know where the fuse box is, but I don't know what switches to pull." She looked at me hopefully. "Do you?"

"No." I was definitely not in the mood for another visit to the Danners' basement.

She sighed. "Then I'll have to wait for my father to come home, I suppose. What were you doing with the crabby Carpeks?"

"Talking," I said. "They have problems." I cocked my head to remind her that Allie was listening, but I needn't have bothered.

"Well, I don't want to hear about *their* problems," April announced. "And I hope my mother and father don't hear about them either. Especially my mother!" She was warning *me* now. "If my mother gets upset again, she'll probably move out for good."

"Don't worry," I snapped. "She won't hear anything from me."

Allie looked from one of us to the other. "Hear

what?" she asked plaintively. "Are you talking about the moonlight man?"

April rolled her eyes.

I had to get away from both of them. "I'm going upstairs to change," I said. "I'm soaked, in case no one noticed."

So now I'm alone here in my bedroom, and I feel like crying, which doesn't happen very often. I keep seeing the moonlight man at the top of the Carpeks' stairs, and I understand, finally, how determined he is. He really does want to drive the Carpeks crazy.

Writing this helps, sort of, but it doesn't change anything. April won't listen; she'd rather go on pretending that what happens next door has nothing to do with the rest of us. And if I tell the Burtons, Mike will turn it into a feature story for the paper.

So whom does that leave? My dad, of course.

I look around this little room, loving it, wondering if I can bear to give it up. Because if I tell him, that's what will happen next. If there's one thing Dad hates, it's "complications."

TWENTY-ONE

A sound like gunshots woke me today. I rolled over in a panic and saw Dad in the doorway looking grim.

"What's wrong?" I kicked off the sheet and jumped out of bed. "Who's shooting? What's happening?"

"The Fourth of July is happening," he said dryly. "What else? You know, fireworks, parades, all that good stuff."

I sank down on the edge of my bed. The Fourth of July was one of my favorite holidays, and I'd forgotten about it. That shows how much time I've spent lately thinking about anything real and fun and *normal*.

"Then today is Mike and Kathy's cookout!" I said, trying to cover up how startled I'd been. "That'll be cool!"

"Sure will," he said, but he didn't sound enthusiastic. And when he came in and sat next to me, I knew it wasn't the Fourth of July we were going to talk about.

"Something's going on, Jenny," he said. "Your sister's downstairs pretending to eat her breakfast and looking as if she's lost her last friend. You're up here jumpy as a kitten. I may not win any ribbons as a single parent, but I know when something's wrong."

I'd meant to have a plan before I actually told him. I wanted to find a calm, convincing way to talk about the moonlight man. If I could do that, maybe together we would figure out what to do. But when I looked at his face, so tight and suspicious, I knew it was way too late for a plan. So I just started in, half awake and with the bang-bang-bang of firecrackers for background.

I started with that first evening in the crescent, when Allie and I saw the moonlight man and his dog in the backyard. I told him about David Tate and Cora Blake and the car accident that happened fifty years ago this week. I described the footsteps and the whistling I've heard when I'm alone in the house, and the car that forced us off the road before it disappeared. I told him about the time we saw Mr. Carpek lying in the backyard and about the way his ladder had fallen over with no one near it. I was just about to describe what had happened at the Carpeks' yesterday afternoon — I'd saved the worst for last! — when he interrupted.

"That's enough!" he said coldly. "It sounds to me as if we've settled down in a nest of lunatics. Ghosts in the backyard, ladders falling over — honestly, Jenny, I thought you were too bright to believe nonsense like that. I thought you *liked* living here!"

"I do!" I exclaimed. "I love it! And so does Allie. This is our perfect place, if we can figure out a way to make David Tate go away. I was going to tell you about him today — I was hoping you'd help."

"Ho, ho," he said, in a way that wasn't one bit funny. "I'll help, all right. I'm going to get you both out of this asylum. One month's notice — that's all it'll take, and we'll be on our way!"

"But we don't have to leave!" I yelled. "I was afraid you'd be like this — that's why I didn't tell you before. You always want to run away. . . ."

I hadn't meant to say that. He looked as if I'd hit him.

"I'm sorry," I whispered, but he shook his head.

"I'm sorry, too," he said and stood up. "I depend

150

on you to help make a home for your sister. She needs to feel safe, and instead she must be scared out of her wits."

He started out of the room and then came back. "Just for the record," he said, "this is *not* a perfect house. The reason you like it so much is because it looks like the house your mother grew up in out in Iowa. We'll find another place that's just as nice. Nicer! And you can bet that next time I'll check out the neighbors before we move in."

I didn't know what he was talking about. "I never saw Mom's house in Iowa," I said. "I've never been to Iowa."

"There's a snapshot somewhere," he said. "It's probably in that box you brought up from the basement." He didn't look quite as angry then, just tired. "You may not remember looking at it, but I'll bet my last dollar that's why you think this place is so great."

After he left, I just sat there, in the blackest mood of my entire life. What I'd worried about most was going to happen. A month or two from now our house would be just a memory. It was so unfair! We'd stayed longer than that in our worst apartment — the one with cockroaches in the kitchen and a leaky toilet.

When I finally made myself get dressed and go downstairs, Dad and Allie were outside. The snapshot of the house in Iowa lay on the kitchen table. I looked at it for a long time and realized I'd seen it many times before. Except for a round flowerbed on the little front lawn, the house in the picture did look exactly like this one. So what! I thought. If that was why I'd loved this place from the first moment, it was a very good reason. Mom had told me wonderful stories about her childhood and the great times she'd had. I know she'd be pleased that we lived in a house like hers.

I was making myself some toast when Allie ran in. If she'd been "scared out of her wits" earlier, she'd gotten over it. "Daddy's going to take us to the parade," she announced. "And to the park for ice cream afterward. Hurry up and eat, Jenny!" She frowned. "Don't you want to go to the parade?"

"Sure, I do," I said. "That's fine with me." I wasn't going to give Dad another chance to say I was spoiling Allie's life.

"Well, then." She could hardly wait.

"Go upstairs and get the suntan lotion," I told her. "Remember what a bad burn you got at the parade last year?"

Newton always has neat parades — bands and floats and tons of people marching. The veterans turn out in their old uniforms, and the Scouts and the high-school cheerleading squad are all there. This year there was even a bunch of little kids from the YMCA gymnastics class. We stood in front of the post office, which is where we've stood every year for as long as I can remember.

For a while I just let the sun wash over me and tried to remember what it had been like when I was Allie's age. But then, during a gap between floats, or a quiet time when no band was playing, I started going over the things Dad and I had said to each other this morning. Maybe it was the Carpeks the moonlight man hated, but David Tate was hurting us, too.

When the last float had passed, we followed the parade to the park, and Allie and I lined up for free ice cream while Dad waited in the shade. A weird thing happened when we went back to him. I suppose it was the sunlight that made the lines in his face so deep, but for a second I didn't recognize him. My own father! He looked as lost and unhappy as I felt.

"No need to go home right away," he said, as we walked back to the car. "Let's drive around for a while."

"We can count flags," Allie suggested. "You count on your side, Jenny, and I'll count on Daddy's side. I bet I'll win."

We drove around the suburbs east of town, down one street after another, counting instead of talking to each other. I knew pretty quickly it wasn't flags Dad was looking for. We kept passing apartment complexes, most of them with FOR RENT signs out in front. At first I pretended not to notice, but after the fourth or fifth one, I couldn't keep still.

"You can tell these are all really expensive," I said. "Lots more than we're paying for our house."

"Not necessarily," Dad said, but he turned south then to the part of town where we used to live. When we passed our old apartment building, there was an APARTMENT AVAILABLE sign fastened to the brick siding.

"Why are we here?" Allie sounded alarmed. "Jeffy and Joy Marie don't live here anymore, Daddy."

"Nobody lives here very long," I told her. "It's just a place to stay until you find something you like better."

Allie was quiet, looking from one of us to the other. "Can we get a dog this summer?" she asked suddenly. "Now that we have a nice house and a big yard?"

Trick question, I thought. She knows something's wrong.

Dad gave me a sideways glance, as if I'd put her up

154

to asking. "Not a good idea," he said. "Our next place may not have room for a dog."

Allie leaned against me. Her question had been answered, and she didn't want to believe it. "Justin has a dog," she said softly. "He's going to bring it to school for Pet Day."

If we moved, Allie probably wouldn't even be going to Justin's school. Dad didn't say anything but drove around awhile longer, then turned into a fast-food place for lunch. "This okay with you?" he asked me.

I said I didn't care. "I just want some soda," I said. I wasn't sulking — at least, I don't think I was — but I was too depressed to be hungry.

Mike had said the cookout would start at five o'clock, and it was a little after that when we drove into the crescent. We'd spent the afternoon at a movie. Dad let Allie choose, and she picked the one with 101 puppies in it. All the way home she talked about how wonderful it would be to have a pet.

When we came out of our garage, Kathy and Mike waved to us from their backyard.

"Welcome!" Kathy shouted. "We've been waiting for you!"

I saw that the three Danners and the Carpeks were

already there, sitting stiffly in plastic chairs. The Burtons' picnic table was covered with a bright red cloth that kept trying to blow away in the breeze. A big flag flapped from the porch rail.

"Let's go," Allie said. She grabbed my hand and started to pull me across the Carpeks' lawn. Dad didn't move. I knew he liked the Burtons and thought Mr. and Mrs. Danner were a couple of airheads. After what I'd told him this morning, he probably didn't even want to look at the Carpeks.

"You have to come," I whispered. "We promised. You'll be the only one who isn't neighborly."

"Neighborly!" He snorted. "Deliver me from neighbors who see spooks around every corner and blame them for all their troubles. To say nothing of scaring my kids half to death!"

"I'm not scared," Allie said, but she drew back a little, remembering, I suppose, that she was going to have to face Mr. Carpek.

"It's okay," I told her. "Dad's coming. This is a party — we'll have fun. Nothing frightening is going to happen here."

Which just shows you how *wrong* a person can be, even when she thinks she's telling the absolute truth!

TWENTY-TWO

"I'll say this," Dad muttered as we crossed the Carpeks' yard, "the Burtons aren't afraid of a challenge. What in the world are they going to do with us all evening?"

I think that was the first time I realized that having a good party might be difficult — even impossible! — depending on your guests. Mr. Carpek sat there glaring straight ahead, his arms folded across his chest as if he dared anyone to make him enjoy himself. Mrs. Carpek's head was bent over her clasped hands as if she were praying. And the Danners weren't much better. Mr. Danner wore a totally bored expression, and

Mrs. Danner's smile seemed frozen in place. She had on a white pantsuit and lots of jewelry, and her eyes darted around as if she expected to see something awful — or disgusting! — at any moment.

April sat by herself, very tall and straight, with a faraway look in her eyes. Sure, she had come to the cookout, but her mind was someplace else. Hearing music, I thought. Or playing it.

And then, of course, Mike and Kathy had us: Dad, who didn't want to come; Allie who was worried about Mr. Carpek; and me — totally depressed because this was a kind of farewell to the crescent for our family, even if our neighbors didn't know it.

But if we were a hopeless bunch of guests, Kathy and Mike didn't seem to care. As soon as we sat down, Mike bounded into the middle of our little semicircle of chairs and dropped a couple of big, bright-colored boxes on the grass.

"Game time!" he announced, like a counselor taking charge of a bunch of sad-sack campers. "Has anybody played boccie ball before?"

"Never heard of it," Mr. Danner said disdainfully. "I'm not a game person."

"It's kind of like bowling," Mike told him. "We roll the balls or toss them to see who can get closest to the goal." He opened one of the boxes and showed us the painted wooden balls.

Mr. Carpek snorted. "I been playing boccie all my life," he grunted. "Don't tell *me* how to play it!"

Mike beamed at him. "Well, that's great!" he exclaimed. "Then you can help Bob learn the fine points."

"I played a few times when I was a kid," Dad said, surprising me. "You'll have to remind me of the rules."

"Glad to," Mike replied. He picked up the box and led the way to the other side of the yard. The men trailed after him, although Mr. Danner took his time getting out of his chair and sighed a lot.

Then it was Kathy's turn to take charge. "These are called Jarts," she announced, opening the second box. Inside were long, steel-tipped arrows with colored fins. A couple of plastic circles lay on top of them.

"The circles are the goals," Kathy explained. "We'll take turns throwing the arrows at them. April, you and Allison and Mrs. Carpek can be Team One. Mrs. Danner and Jenny and I are Team Two. Just be sure to stay well behind the person who's throwing — the arrows are heavy, and we don't want anyone to get hurt."

Mrs. Carpek and Mrs. Danner looked as if they were already hurting, but they lined up with the rest of us while Kathy demonstrated how to hold a Jart and toss it.

More than ever, I want to be exactly like Kathy someday. Between them, she and Mike managed to get all of us on our feet. Even more amazing, once we started playing, everyone seemed to enjoy it. Even Mrs. Carpek! She didn't stop looking worried, but once, when Allie made a good throw, she actually said, "Good for you, missy."

As for Mrs. Danner, the game changed her amazingly. Her first throw landed the Jart in the middle of the goal, and after that her phony smile disappeared.

"I'm really good at this!" she exclaimed each time it was her turn, and she sounded so surprised and pleased that the rest of us — even April — cheered.

April was good at it, too, without trying very hard. Allie and I were only fair — maybe we tried *too* hard. It didn't matter. By the time we'd played three games, we were all cheering the good throws and offering advice after a bad one. Across the yard, the men were laughing and kidding one another, too.

After about an hour, I saw Mike leave the boccie game to put hamburgers and ears of corn on the grill.

Then Kathy went into the house to bring out the rest of the food, and I followed her to help.

"That was neat!" I said.

She reached over and patted my hand. "I grew up in a very friendly neighborhood," she said. "And I do think everybody's having a good time — except maybe you, Jenny. Why is that?"

I wanted to blurt out, "We're moving!" but I couldn't. "Nothing special," I lied. "Tell you later." *When I can say it without crying.*

Mike set a card table close to the picnic table, and we all stuffed ourselves with hamburgers, corn, potato chips, and fruit salad, while darkness settled around us. The dessert was perfect for the Fourth of July — red-frosted cupcakes and vanilla ice cream with blueberries.

When we were through eating, Mike brought out a guitar. "I shouldn't do this when we have a *real* musician at the party," he said, smiling at April. "But if anyone feels like singing . . ."

He strummed a few notes, and soon everyone except the Carpeks joined in. Mrs. Carpek kept glancing around the yard uneasily. Once in a while she clutched her husband's arm, but he ignored her.

Mike played folk songs and tunes from Broadway

musicals first, and then he switched to patriotic songs in honor of the Fourth. We sang "Yankee Doodle" and "God Bless America," and we were just finishing "America the Beautiful" when the first rocket whistled up from the schoolyard on the other side of the woods. A shower of blue and silver burst across the sky.

That ended the singing. We settled down to watch, as one rocket after another spread an umbrella of red or blue or gold or silver above the treetops. I saw Mike reach for Kathy's hand, and I knew what they were thinking: This was the perfect ending for their party.

But then it wasn't perfect, after all. Suddenly, the soft breeze turned cool and became a real wind. The treetops began to toss and dip like waves in a storm. Behind us the Burtons' flag flapped with a noise like gunshot.

"What's this?" Mr. Danner demanded, sounding annoyed. Mrs. Carpek screamed, "Arthur! My shoe!"

We all stared at the glittering blue ash that danced on her toe. Mr. Carpek started to get up, but Dad moved faster. He brushed the fiery speck away, but another took its place. Then a whole shower of blue and gold sparks settled on his shoulders. Mike jumped to sweep them off, and a moment later we were all scrambling for cover. The wind blew a storm of hot, sparkling ash all over the yard.

"What are those fools in the schoolyard doing?" Mr. Danner yelled. "Don't they know —"

"I'm sure they don't," Mike shouted back. "This wind came out of nowhere. Just stand back, folks — we'll be okay."

"Look at my pantsuit," Mrs. Danner wailed. "Burned spots all over!"

I searched for Allie and saw that Dad had his arms wrapped around her. They were on the porch steps, with the Carpeks huddled close to them. When I saw the terror on the old people's faces, the shower of burning ash stopped being an unexpected adventure and turned into something much worse.

"Go away!" Mrs. Carpek screamed, above the roar of the wind and the banging of the rockets. "Leave us alone! It wasn't our fault!" Dad looked at her in amazement.

"Go!" she shrieked again. "Leave us alone!"

The gale died down a little then, almost as if it were obeying her. The rain of sparks moved away from us.

"That's better!" Mike shouted. "We're okay!"

But we weren't. Almost at once, the wind picked up again, and this time it came from every direction, gathering the sparks high in the air. As we stared, a tornado of fire and light moved across the Burtons' yard and behind their garage. When it reached the Carpeks' lawn next door, it billowed forward, and the whole burning torrent poured down on the roof of their house.

"That's bad!" Mr. Danner exclaimed. "Those old shingles are dry as paper! We've got to get the fire department up here!"

Kathy dashed into their house, and Mike headed toward the garage. "I'll get the hose," he shouted. "We can keep the roof wet till help comes."

Mr. Danner and Mr. Carpek hurried after him, and Dad pushed Allie into my arms. "I'm going over to the schoolyard and tell them what's happening," he said grimly. "If a fire starts here it could take this whole row of houses!"

My heart stopped when he said that. Allie began to cry, and Mrs. Carpek cried, too — horrible choking sobs. I heard her say something about "fifty years" and "wicked boy" and I thought she mumbled something about "wedding," too. Then Mrs. Danner took her hand and drew her down the porch steps. "Come on, dear," she said kindly. "Maybe we can give them a hand with the hose."

"We have a hose, too," I said to April. "Let's get it."

She grabbed Allie's other hand, and the three of us raced around the Burtons' house and across the front yards to our driveway. The wind was even louder now, and I could smell something burning.

Hoses won't help! I thought. The fire department won't help! It's too late! Mrs. Carpek's mention of a wedding had horrified me. Was the Fourth of July the date David Tate and Cora Blake had chosen for their wedding?

We dragged the curled-up hose out of our garage and around to the faucet at the back of the house. The burning smell was much stronger there, and when we looked up we saw smoke rising from the Carpeks' roof in four or five different places. I struggled to fasten the hose to the faucet — the threads were nearly worn out — and at last water poured out of the nozzle. April held it as high as she could and aimed the stream at the Carpeks' roof. The water didn't reach much above the eaves, but she kept it shooting upward anyway, even when the wind blew the spray back in her face.

I remembered the ladder propped in the corner of our garage and was about to go back for it when Allie grabbed my arm.

"Jenny!" she squealed. "Look!" She pointed toward the back of our yard.

He was there. The trees bent crazily in the wind, bright sparks hurtled toward the roof, the tire-swing flew back and forth like a pendulum, and the only thing not moving in the entire yard was the dark shape of the moonlight man.

TWENTY-THREE

I think that when you're *horribly* frightened, your brain must work like a video camera, recording every detail. Right now if I close my eyes I can hear the bang and hiss of rockets, the bellowing of the wind, and the shouts of the men on the other side of the Carpeks' house. I can see that beautiful rain of fire and the trees bowing beneath it as if they were about to break. I can see Kathy's red paper tablecloth sailing across our yard. Clearest of all, I see the ghost of David Tate. He was as real as the light that shone over him and through him.

"That can't be," April said in a scared, little-girl voice. She didn't drop the hose, but it wobbled wildly. Maybe seeing him was even worse for her than it was for Allie and me, since she'd never let herself believe.

The moonlight man stood with his feet apart, his arms at his sides, and his head tipped back to watch the Carpeks' smoking roof. I couldn't see his eyes, but I could make out the lower part of his face and the line of his jaw. He was smiling.

"What'll we do, Jenny?" Allie whispered. She'd moved behind me, but she didn't run.

I reached back and pulled her close. "Don't know," I said. The terrifying smile said a lot. David Tate was destroying the Carpeks' home, because he believed they'd destroyed his own chance for happiness. He didn't care who else got hurt.

"Someone should try to stop him," I mumbled.

April did drop the hose then. Water splashed across our ankles in an icy stream. "That's the dumbest thing I ever heard of!" she gasped. "You wouldn't dare!"

"I said *someone* should," I told her. But I knew who it was going to be. Even if we weren't going to be living in it much longer, I had to try to save our house.

I moved away from Allie. She said, "Don't!" but I kept on walking toward the woods.

168

I'd taken a few steps when a blast of water hit me between the shoulder blades. I turned around and saw April pointing the hose at me. Her face was white and resentful. She'd looked that same way the night she let me go into her basement alone to look for the crying woman. *Don't try to make me feel guilty*, the look said. *Just because I'm not like you. Just because I've got better things to do than try to be a hero . . .*

"You're crazy!" she shouted. "You're the craziest person I know!" Allie jumped at her, knocking the hose aside, and I kept on walking.

I was close enough now to see David Tate's little dog curled up at his feet. The dog watched me, but his master didn't turn until I was a few feet away. I think I surprised him; all his attention had been centered on the Carpeks' roof. His smile vanished, and he stared at me, a hard look that sent goose bumps up and down my arms.

I opened my mouth but no words came out. This was a ghost, for goodness' sake! A dead person! And he was close enough to touch me!

I took a step backward. "I-I'm sorry," I stammered. "I'm sorry for your grief."

Up close, David Tate was young and handsome. He didn't speak, but I sort of *felt* a reply from him, a warning, maybe. Then he looked upward again. I looked, too, and saw more smoke drifting from the Carpeks' shingles. Close to the chimney, a tongue of fire leaped into the air.

"Listen! Please!" I tried again. "I know you think those people spoiled your plans to get married. Maybe you blame them for your accident, too. But that was a long time ago, and now they're old and you're scaring them to death. If you burn their house — if you burn all our houses — it won't change the way things are. It won't help!"

The smile came back. Oh, yes, he was saying, it *would* help. He was like a little kid, determined to get even. It was stupid to think I could make him feel sorry for the Carpeks.

Maybe there was another way to get his attention. "I know about Cora," I said. "You must have loved each other very much." He glanced back at me, and for that moment the firestorm seemed to lessen. It was enough to keep me talking. "Cora must have been really sad when she came home from California and found you'd been killed. Did you know she kept her wedding dress in a big box locked away in her basement? It was in a special place where she could look at it but no one else could see it. All those years when she lived in that house alone, I bet she looked at it a thousand times. She's sick now, but I'm sure she still loves you and dreams about the dress. Sometimes the dreams are so real that her spirit leaves the place where she's staying and comes back to her house to look at it again."

His eyes bored into me, and I talked faster. "She must feel close to you here," I said. "She misses you as much as you miss her."

The wind had almost stopped. He was thinking about Cora and how much he'd loved her, not about how much he hated the Carpeks. If I could keep his attention long enough . . .

Sirens wailed in the distance, and someone — Kathy, I think — shouted, "They're coming!" David Tate turned away from me fast, as if he were waking up from a dream. He looked at the roof, and the wind began to rise again, fanning the flames that danced around the chimney.

"Please!" I said. "Please stop!"

This time the warning in his eyes was as clear as if he'd said it aloud. *Get out!* In another second I would have been running back to Allie and April as fast as I could go. But before I could move, something else happened — the strangest thing of all.

The moonlight man's eyes narrowed, then widened. The rage drained out of his face, and in its place was disbelief. I whirled around and saw my father standing still as a statue at the entrance to the path through the woods. Beyond him, in the center of the Danners' yard, was a girl. She was smiling and radiant in a long, white dress. A circle of flowers rested on her smooth, dark hair, and she held a nosegay of violets.

David Tate stepped forward. I tried to get out of his way, but my legs wouldn't do what I told them to. I remember sitting down — hard — and then as he walked through me I felt a wave of joy, his joy, like nothing I've ever felt before.

I heard Dad yell, "Jenny!" and I heard Allie crying, but they seemed very far away. I watched the moonlight man drift across the lawn with his dog at his heels. When he reached the girl, he took her hand and they moved together into the shadows. The wind went with them.

Gradually, I became aware of grass prickling my elbows and the backs of my knees. There was smoke everywhere and the crackling of burning shingles overhead.

"You can stop the fire now!" I shouted after the moonlight man, or I thought I did. But Dad says I fainted as I fell. He says I didn't shout anything at all.

TWENTY-FOUR

"**G**o home and lie down," Dad ordered. "And take Allie with you. I don't want her underfoot while the fire department's here. I'll stay with the others till this thing's under control."

He walked away quickly, before I could ask how long he'd been standing there at the edge of the woods. Actually, I didn't want to talk right then any more than he did. I was sure there was something important I had to do; I just couldn't remember what it was.

"Did you see the girl?" Allie asked, her eyes wide

with excitement as we went into the house. "There was a moonlight girl, Jenny!"

"I saw her," I said, and then, of course, I remembered what the important thing was. I looked up the number of the Southridge Care Center and asked to talk to the nurse who cared for Cora Blake.

It took three or four minutes, with lots of voices murmuring at the other end of the line, but finally someone picked up the phone. She said she was the social worker in charge of Cora Blake's case and asked if I was a member of the Blake family. Then she said she was sorry to have to tell me that Miss Blake had passed over in her sleep this afternoon.

I'd never heard anyone say "passed over" before, but it sounded right for Cora Blake. I knew for a fact that she'd passed over from being sad to being happy and I was glad for her. So was Allie, when I told her about the poor, sick lady we'd tried to visit.

She thought it over, putting the pieces together. "So now there are two ghosts," she said finally. "And the dog makes three."

"Only I don't think they'll be around here any more," I told her. "Now that they have each other."

"Good!" Allie said. "I just wish . . ."

I knew what she wished, but the look on Dad's face

when he told us to go inside made me sure we might as well stop wishing. Whatever he'd seen, standing there in the path, he hadn't liked it.

We wandered from room to room, staying close to the front windows most of the time to watch the firemen work. They dragged long loops of hose from one of the trucks, while Mr. and Mrs. Carpek scurried back and forth, getting in the way. Once a fireman bumped into Mrs. Carpek, nearly knocking her over. He shouted, and Kathy came running to lead her away.

Then April appeared between the houses. She walked like a queen through all the confusion, just the way she'd walked the day we watched her and her family move in. I felt really sad, because that day as she walked toward us I thought we might become best friends. Tonight, when she passed our house without a sideways glance, I knew she'd put us right out of her head, along with the moonlight man and his bride.

I'd been right that first day when I said her best friend just might be her violin. A few minutes passed, and then she began to play. The sound was lovely, soaring over the firemen's racket like a song from another world.

We listened for a while, and then Allie made one of those remarks that make me want to hug her and laugh at the same time. "There's still one empty house up here," she said matter-of-factly. "The one next to Mike and Kathy. Maybe some neat kids will move in there. Maybe they won't play the violin."

An hour and a half passed before the firemen packed up and left. As soon as they were gone, Allie and I went out the back door and looked up at the Carpeks' roof. We couldn't see much in the dark, but there was one very black patch near the chimney that I thought must be a hole. Water dripped from the eaves.

"Jenny! Allison! Come over here." It was Kathy, with Mrs. Danner, sitting at the picnic table.

"The others have gone upstairs to see what can be done until the roofers can come," Kathy explained when we joined them. "Are you okay, Jenny? Your father said you weren't feeling well."

I told her I was fine, and she looked relieved. "I was afraid it might be something you ate."

"I'm sure it was nerves," Mrs. Danner said. "I know I'm still shaking like a leaf."

"Your father says he had a hard time convincing the men in charge of the fireworks that there was any danger," Kathy said. "From the platform where they were setting off the rockets, it apparently looked as if the sparks were fading before they came anywhere near the ground. Isn't that odd? And there was no wind in the schoolyard — only here, over the Carpeks' house." There was a question in her voice, and I felt her looking at me.

"It certainly *is* odd!" Mrs. Danner exclaimed. "And very unlikely! I think they were being careless and don't want to admit it."

Someday I'll tell you, Kathy, I thought. First, I'll make Mike promise not to write about it in the paper, and then I'll tell you what really happened at your cookout.

We sat awhile longer in the dark listening to April play. Then Dad, Mike, and Mr. Danner came out of the Carpeks' house.

"The old folks are exhausted," Mr. Danner said. "After Bill here tacked a tarp across the hole in their attic, they just sort of collapsed. Wanted us to thank you for the party, Kathy." He chuckled. "You know, I can almost believe they were having a good time until the fireworks started."

"Of course they had a good time," Mrs. Danner said. "We all did. We're lucky to have the Burtons for neighbors."

Everyone — including Dad — said that was true,

but I could feel him wanting to go home. The Danners were ready to leave, too, and soon we were walking together across the lawn.

"See you, Bill," Mr. Danner said, as if he and Dad had been best friends for years. Mrs. Danner patted Allie's shoulder and said, "You're a sweet little girl." And then we were alone.

I'd turned on the little lamp next to the stove when Allie and I went outside, and the kitchen looked cozy in its soft glow. Dad filled the kettle to make instant coffee, and I put the cookie jar in the middle of the table. He told Allie it was past her bedtime, but when she said she wasn't sleepy, he didn't argue.

"So tell me, Jenny," he said slowly, "who did you think you were talking to out there tonight?" His voice shook.

"That was David Tate," I said. "The girl was his fiancée, Cora Blake. I told you about them, Dad. Now you've seen them yourself."

"I don't know what I saw!" he exploded. He splashed boiling water into a mug and slumped into a chair.

"I think this must have been the fiftieth anniversary of their wedding day," I went on. "Only the wedding never happened, because Cora's folks took her away, and then David was killed in a car accident. Cora died at the Southridge Care Center this afternoon."

Dad blinked. "Now how in the world would you know that?"

"I called."

He shook his head. "I don't believe any of this," he said. "I don't care what it looked like out there — I don't believe it. But if there *is* something supernatural going on, I don't want you girls anywhere near it. What were you saying to that *thing*, anyway?"

"She was telling the moonlight man to stop trying to burn down the Carpeks' house," Allie said, watching him anxiously. "April squirted the hose at her, but she went anyway. And she made him stop."

I waited for another explosion, but Dad just stared at us.

"It was seeing Cora that made him stop," I said. "Now that they're together, I'm pretty sure he won't stay around here any more. The Carpeks won't have to be afraid, and neither will we."

"You're pretty sure," Dad repeated. "My daughter, the expert on ghosts." He rubbed his forehead. Then he said something that really surprised me. "Jenny's going to spend her life taking care of the whole world." I had the strangest feeling that he was talking to my mother. "She has a talent for it — must be inherited, and not from me."

Allie ran around the table and threw her arms around his waist. "We aren't going to move, are we?" she asked, but he just patted her shoulder and said, "We'll talk about it tomorrow. Right now I'm too tired to think straight."

So maybe you're wondering why I feel so good tonight. Two reasons, really.

First, I never once thought that taking care of people might be a talent — like playing the violin. If it is, I'm glad I have it. And second, when Allie asked about the house, Dad said, "We'll talk about it tomorrow." That may not sound encouraging to you, but it's a lot better than what I expected. Maybe tonight he enjoyed having neighbors, and being one, as much as I did. At least he didn't say, "Start packing."

I've decided that tomorrow morning I'll give him this journal and ask him to read it. I know I told you at the beginning that he never listens to what I think is important, but maybe this time is going to be different.

Allie thinks it is. When I went to her room to say good night her eyes were closed. I started to tiptoe away, but then it turned out she wasn't asleep after all. "Jenny," she said, "Sammy wants to know how soon we can get a dog."